ELVIS AND THE MEMPHIS MAMBO MURDERS

"Let's look at the river, Elvis."

Apparently everybody else has the same idea because we can't even get close to the ornate, Italian-style concrete balustrade. Still, the view of the Mississippi is magnificent.

"Isn't this peaceful?"

The words are no sooner out of my mouth than there's an explosion of flapping wings. Feathers fly, ducks squawk, and a high-pitched scream rips the air. Crowd control vanishes.

While I drag Elvis out of the melee, I glance around to see if I can locate the source of this near riot.

When I do, my stomach turns. I open my mouth to yell, but somebody beats me to it.

"It's Babs Mabry Mims!"

Not anymore.

What's left of her is plastered on the sidewalk thirteen stories below . . .

Books by Peggy Webb

ELVIS AND THE DEARLY DEPARTED

ELVIS AND THE GRATEFUL DEAD

ELVIS AND THE MEMPHIS MAMBO MURDERS

ELVIS AND THE TROPICAL DOUBLE TROUBLE

Published by Kensington Publishing Corporation

ELVIS
and the
Memphis
Mambo Murders

Peggy Webb

KENSINGTON BOOKS
http://www.kensingtonbooks.com

Kensington Books are published by

Kensington Publishing Corp.
119 West 40th Street
New York, NY 10018

ISBN-13: 978-0-7582-2594-8
ISBN-10: 0-7582-2594-6

First Hardcover Printing: October 2010
First Mass Market Printing: September 2011

10 9 8 7 6 5 4 3 2 1

Printed in the United States of America

In celebration of Elvis Presley,
who would have been 75 this year.

Elvis' Opinion #1 on Graceland, Road Trips, and Uncontrollable Geriatrics

I hate to leave my best friend behind (Jarvetis' redbone hound Trey) not to mention Ann-Margret and my new progeny (more on that subject later), but it's not every day I get a chance to return to Graceland. If I could get word up to Memphis I'm coming back home, they'd roll out the red carpet, probably get in the kitchen and rustle up my favorite peanut butter and banana sandwiches. But Callie (that's my human mom) says basset hounds don't use telephones. I'd argue with her (after all, I'm a dog of superior intelligence, not to mention savoir faire), but these days she's having a hard time sorting out her feelings.

Personally, I know she's still in love with my human daddy, Jack Jones (her almost-ex), but Champ is building a good case for himself as Jack's replacement, and Callie's confused. I'm doing what I can for Jack.

Don't get me wrong. Champ's a good guy and would be one of the best vets in the country if it weren't for that ridiculous, uppity Siamese cat he keeps on the premises. There's no way I'm letting that cat horn in on my territory.

Usually Jack's around to protect our turf, but the last time Champ called, Jack was in Africa doing things I'd have to kill you over if I told you. Much as I hated to disappoint my human mom, I peed on every one of her shoes so she had to cancel the date.

It took a while to clean them off and dry them out, but she didn't even scold me. That's Callie. An "Angel Flying Too Close to the Ground," to borrow from fellow singer Willie Nelson. She tries to take care of everybody, which is the reason we're headed to Memphis in the first place.

Ruby Nell (Callie's mama) and her best friend, Fayrene, entered a regional dance competition, and Callie's going along to make sure nothing happens. You might think you wouldn't have to worry about women in their senior years, but you'd be mistaken. Excitement follows Ruby Nell Valentine the way it did me when I was wearing black leather, crooning gold, and making girls swoon. There's no telling what those two feisty geriatrics are up to.

That's the main reason Charlie (Callie's uncle and guiding force for the entire Valentine family) is staying behind in Tupelo. He says it's to run his funeral home and keep an eye on things here in Mooreville, but I'm a dog with mismatched ears. I hear what I hear. Charlie's not too happy with the prospect of Ruby Nell doing the mambo all over Memphis with her so-called dance partner, and he's not fixing to go along and watch.

But that's all I'm saying on the subject. I'm a dog of discretion. I know how to keep family secrets.

And speaking of discretion, there's cousin Lovie (Charlie's daughter), who doesn't even know the meaning of the word. Which is one of the reasons I'm glad she's going with us. The other is that she knows a dog needs plenty of fat-loaded snacks, no matter what kind of diet his human mom has put him on. Now there's a woman who sympathizes with a slightly portly King in a dog suit. Lovie's got plenty of curves, herself.

Currently, her goal is to throw some kerosene on the fire she's been trying to light under the love of her life. Rocky Malone is the old-fashioned, steady type and not the kind of man to be swayed by Lovie's antics, but I'm keeping my opinions on romance to myself.

Listen, I want Lovie in Memphis and I don't want her mad at me. She's my only hope of getting to sneak out of the Peabody Hotel for a rendezvous with a rack of ribs.

And speaking of ribs, I think I'll mosey into the back yard through the doggie door and make sure that mealy-mouthed cocker spaniel pretender to my throne knows better than to steal my ham bones while I'm gone. I may look like God's gift to female dogs, but I'm not above vengeance. Especially with Hoyt. If I didn't have such a generous heart, I'd say Callie should have left him behind the garbage can.

But that's Callie, always taking in strays. And that's me. In spite of my "Don't Step on my Blue

Suede Shoes" attitude, I'm just "A Big Hunk o' Love."

Wait a minute. What's this I hear? Callie at the back door calling my name.

"Elvis, are you terrorizing poor Hoyt?" I give my human mom an innocent grin that fools her completely, then pretend to be helping Hoyt bury the bone. She comes out to scratch my ears. A lesser dog would feel ashamed of his deception, but I don't. I'm a worldwide icon: I thrive on adoration. "There are plenty of bones to go around. Come on, boy. Lovie's waiting. Let's go to Memphis."

Well bless'a my soul. That's music to my ears. I always did shine on road trips.

Chapter 1

Hairdos, Famous Ducks, and Double Trouble

Wouldn't you know? When we registered for the competition, the first dance Mama signed up for was the mambo. Most women her age would be content with the waltz or a sedate two step. But naturally, Ruby Nell Valentine wants to shake herself all over the floor—with Mr. Whitenton, no less.

I wish she wouldn't encourage him. He's already acting like more than her dance partner.

Thinking about it drives me crazy, so I'm going to be like Scarlett; I'll think about it tomorrow. Right now I've got to unpack my bag.

Lovie and I are sharing a room on the fourth floor of the grand old Peabody Hotel. While I arrange my cute designer shoes on the closet shelf—my only extravagance unless you count the gazillion tons of cat and dog food I buy to feed my rescued menagerie—my rabble-rouser cousin and loyal-to-the-bone best friend is throwing her things into the closet in messy wads.

"Lovie, your clothes will get wrinkled."

She strikes a pose. "With this body? I've got enough curves to fill out every wrinkle in the Grand Canyon." She continues to toss clothes into the closet, ignoring hangers.

I don't know why, but this comforts me. Lovie will never change. She'll always be the lovable, irascible, outrageous woman who can make me laugh, comfort me when I'm blue, pick me up and carry me when I stumble and fall.

"Do you think Mama and Mr. Whitenton are doing anything besides dancing?"

"I hope so. Aunt Ruby Nell's got it and I hope she's flaunting it."

Strike *comfort me.*

"If you're trying to worry me, you've succeeded."

"You worry too much. Loosen up. We're here for some fun."

Maybe *she* is, but I'm here to watchdog Mama. It's not the little things I worry about—gambling with my money and dancing with the wrong man. It's the big ones—letting the wrong man steal her farm as well as her heart.

My phone rings and it's Mama. I swear she can read minds.

"Callie, come up to my room and make me beautiful."

"Mama, you're already beautiful." I'm proud to say that's true. And though she gets into trouble with aggravating regularity, I'd rather have a mother who is fit and feisty than one who sits home feeling sorry for herself. "I just colored and cut your hair yesterday."

Mama changes her hair color more often than I change my Airwick room freshener. It's easy for her since I own the best little beauty shop in Mooreville—population slightly less than the size of the Calvary Baptist Church's congregation over in Tupelo. But don't let size fool you. I pride myself on giving my customers New York styles.

Actually, the bank and I own Hair.Net, but that's a whole 'nother story.

There's a dead silence at the other end of the phone line.

"Mama, are you still there?"

"I'm here, Callie, and that's all right." Mama's tone says she means just the opposite. "If you don't want to fix my hair, I can make an appointment downstairs and get on the dance floor wearing a Memphis hairdo."

Like the gamblers in the old Westerns Lovie and I watch, I know when to hold 'em and when to fold 'em. I say to Mama, "I'll be right there," then hang up the telephone and rummage in my bag for my hair styling tools.

"Here, you'll need this." Lovie tosses me a bag of potato chips from the stash she's storing in the closet. The amount of food she travels with would be mind boggling if you didn't know she loves to cook. Her state of the art kitchen is always filled with goodies, even when they're not for some posh event she's catering in Tupelo.

Plopping onto the bed nearest the door, she opens a bag for herself. "What kind of blackmail did Aunt Ruby Nell use?"

While I tell her, I rip into my chips, never mind that we had big chunks of her chocolate cherry cake after we checked in less than an hour ago. To celebrate the beginning of our girls' weekend out, Lovie said, though I don't know how much celebrating I'll have time for. I'll be too busy making sure Mama's dance partner keeps his hands where they belong.

Not that Thomas Whitenton is a bad person. But Mama has hardly looked at another man since Daddy died. I don't want her throwing away twenty-seven years of caution on a man who smacks his lips at the end of every sentence.

Elvis stands at my feet and gives me such a mournful look, I relent and hand him a chip. One won't wreck his diet. And he *is* irresistible.

"Lovie, are you going to stay here or do you want to go up with me?"

"And let Rocky think I have nothing better to do than hang around in hotel rooms?"

"I don't think he's like that. Didn't he tell you to have a good time on this trip?"

"Which is exactly what I intend to do. But wait till word filters down to Mexico I'm the sensation of Memphis. He'll change his tune."

I'd ask Lovie how word is going to filter to Rocky on an archeological dig in the depths of a jungle, but I already know. She's the one who will do the filtering.

I wish she'd settle down and realize he's crazy about her, even if he is too old-fashioned to find her Holy Grail (her words, not mine). But who am I to give love advice? My own love life is as tangled up as kudzu on a ditch bank.

"What are you going to do while I'm gone?" I

ask her. Nothing as ordinary as shopping, I can guarantee.

"I thought I'd take Elvis to the lobby to watch the parade of the Peabody ducks."

The parade of ducks began in 1930 when the general manager of the Peabody Hotel returned from a hunting trip and put three English ducks in the Grand Lobby's fountain as a prank. They were such a hit that the twice-a-day parade of ducks was initiated and became a tradition. The duck master leads his charges from their penthouse pond to the elevator where they ride to the lobby. With a John Philip Sousa march playing and crowds cheering, the ducks stroll across a red carpet and walk a tiny duck staircase to the beautiful travertine marble fountain that makes the lobby in this grand old hotel look like a small piazza in Italy.

"Keep him out of trouble, Lovie. It took an act of Congress to get him here."

The Peabody Hotel has a strict *no pets* policy. After begging and pleading to no avail, I was getting ready to leave Elvis at home with Uncle Charlie, but all of a sudden the hotel manager called and said they were making an exception.

Uncle Charlie told me it was Jack's doing, though I'd have figured it out. Everything that gets mysteriously straightened out, fixed up, and smoothed over is Jack's doing.

I have never known exactly what my almost-ex does. If you ask his profession, he always says *international consultant*, which tells exactly nothing.

I confronted him the night before I left for

Memphis (and he left for heaven knows where). We were in my bedroom. A huge tactical error on my part. He'd just broken and entered, but don't think I'm fixing to work up a wad of guilt over that. We *are* still husband and wife. Sort of.

"Where do you get all your power, Jack?"

"A hundred push-ups a day. Do you want me to show you again?"

"You stay on your side of the bed, Jack Jones." It's hard to be huffy when you're not wearing clothes. "I just want to know what you do."

"You're the only woman who does, Callie."

"Oh, hush up." I grabbed my robe and prissed myself to the other side of the room. It helped, but not much. "I mean what you do for a living."

"I've told you."

I got so mad I said a word (only not the kind Lovie would say). If you want to know the truth, I said *poot*, which made Jack laugh and made me feel guilty. What if I had been pregnant and my unborn child had heard? I'd feel like a toad, not to mention an unfit mother.

"I mean it, Jack. I want to know the truth."

He grabbed his jeans, and I thought he was going to walk out without a word. Instead he stalked over and put his big hands on my shoulders in the way that makes me feel fragile and protected and vulnerable all at the same time.

"You deserve the truth, Cal." His favorite ploy to sidetrack me is a kiss, so I braced myself. Instead he said, "I work for The Company, and that's all I can tell you."

He headed toward the door and I knew I wouldn't

get another word out of him. I didn't press the issue, but I didn't let him get the last word, either.

"You can forget what happened tonight, Jack. I want you to sign those divorce papers, and I mean it." He didn't even answer.

As soon as I heard the front door slam, I looked up The Company on the Internet but I didn't find a single reference. I sat in front of my computer for a long, time feeling chilled, and it had nothing to do with fall.

For goodness sake, even with leaves littering the ground, October in the Deep South still feels like summer.

Now I grab the tools of my trade and head for the elevator and Mama's room on the tenth floor. She's sitting at a gorgeous Queen Anne desk filing her fingernails.

"Where's Fayrene?" I ask.

"Next door."

The words are no sooner out of her mouth than the connecting door opens. I'm all prepared to greet Fayrene, but who should stroll in? None other than Thomas Whitenton. Holding a pair of Mama's shoes. I could spit.

He's so proud of himself he doesn't even see me sitting there like a gathering storm.

"Ruby Nell, where do you want me to put these?" When he notices me, he has the good grace to turn red. Only good Southern upbringing keeps me from snatching the shoes and telling him to keep his mitts off Mama and her stuff.

"In my closet." Mama doesn't blink an eye, just sits there like he's not holding evidence of hanky panky. If I think about it too much, I'm liable to get my first gray hair, so I don't. As a stylist, I strive to set the standard for hair beauty.

Mr. Whitenton mumbles something that sounds like *hello* but could be *goodbye*, then hurries back to his room. A guilty action if I ever saw one.

But I'm not even going to ask what he's doing with her shoes and why they have connecting doors. When Mama wants to keep things from you, you could put her through the Spanish Inquisition and she still wouldn't tell you the truth.

I decide to take the roundabout approach. "Why aren't you rooming with Fayrene?"

"That's my business."

I'd beg to differ since I'm the one subsidizing her trip, but I'm partial to peace. I just take out my natural bristle brush and start brushing her hair.

The upside is that Mama's dancing habit is much cheaper than her gambling habit. At the rate I'm saving money, I can hire a manicurist, at least part time. The only problem is finding somebody to fit smoothly into Mooreville society. Translated, that's my beauty shop, Mooreville Feed and Seed, the video store, and Gas, Grits, and Guts—our one and only convenience store, owned by Fayrene and her husband, Jarvetis Johnson.

Another reason I don't confront Mama about the telltale connecting door is that I really would like a peaceful weekend. I need to sit back and breathe, relax, and think about which direction I'm going.

It's funny how I can be so certain of the future of Hair.Net (first a manicurist, then a tanning bed and spa) and so uncertain of my personal future. I know what I want: a home, a husband and children to love. The problem is, I don't know how I'm going to achieve that ideal.

A part of me wants to go backward and try to fix whatever went wrong with Jack. (How do you forget seven years of marriage?) But another part wants to move forward with Champ. He's uncomplicated and totally reliable and very good looking in a burnished blond sort of way. All the things Jack is not.

Not that Jack's not handsome. He is, but in a dark, dangerous way.

You'd think the choice would be simple. But it appears I'm the kind of woman who can't resist putting her hand in the fire.

"Callie, do you think this color makes me look younger?" Mama fluffs her hair and turns to view herself in the mirror.

I'm relieved to be jerked out of my problems and into Mama's vanities.

"At least fifteen years," I tell her, which is no lie.

Mama hugs me, and I figure you can't get a better start to a relaxing weekend than that. After wishing her good luck at tonight's dance competition, I head toward the elevator to join Lovie and Elvis in the lobby. If I'm lucky I might catch the tail end of the duck parade.

I'm just getting in the elevator when my cell phone rings. It's Lovie.

"Callie, come quick. Elvis is in the fountain."

"Is he hurt?"

"No, it looks like he's trying to steal the show from the Peabody ducks. But hurry. He's creating a sensation and I can't get him out."

So much for my quiet weekend. When you think about it, though, tranquility is highly overrated.

Chapter 2

Memorable Performances, Mama's Mambo, and Murder

I hurry from the elevator hoping to get Elvis out of the fountain before the manager notices and throws us all out. A huge crowd hampers my progress. Fortunately I'm tall enough to see over many of them, especially in my red Kate Spade sling-back heels.

Listen, just because I've been traveling is no reason to let beauty and style slip. I'm in an elegant, historic national landmark as well as one of the ritziest hotels in the South—Tennessee's answer to the Paris Ritz and the London Savoy. I'm not about to let anybody say folks from Mooreville, Mississippi, population 651 and suburb of the King's Tupelo birthplace, don't know style from a cow patty.

Craning my neck, I search for Lovie. She's usually easy to spot. A hundred-and-ninety-pound bombshell with abundant red hair, she stands out. Not today, though. In this milling, chattering crowd, my dearest friend and cohort in everything that matters is nowhere to be seen.

She's probably bending over the fountain trying to coax my dog to come out. If I were the kind of woman to ignore manners, I'd barge through, stepping on toes without even apologizing.

While I'm saying *Pardon me, I'm sorry* for the fifteenth time, a woman shouts, "Look! She's in!" There's a spattering of applause followed by a few catcalls.

This can't be good. I burst through the wall of human flesh, then screech to a halt.

Holy cow! The duck master is wringing his hands, Elvis is paddling around wearing his basset grin, and Lovie is upended in the fountain mooning Memphis. All you can see of her are flailing legs and more black lace than even she would care to show in public.

"Hold on, Lovie," I shout. "I'm coming."

No use ruining a pair of Kate Spades. I'm kicking off my shoes when a couple of long, lanky teenage boys step into the fountain and pluck Lovie out. She comes up sputtering and says a word that threatens to shatter every piece of crystal in the Peabody.

"It's only water, Lovie." I hand her a lipstick-smeared tissue from my purse. She looks at it askance, but starts swabbing her face anyhow.

"If I'd wanted total immersion, I'd have called John the Baptist."

Leave it to Lovie to upgrade her shenanigans with religious icons. Still muttering words I hope nobody else hears, she wrings water out of her skirt while I try to coax Elvis from the fountain.

The crowd on my right parts of its own accord, which can mean only one thing. Somebody important is heading this way. My guess would be the hotel manager. The only thing worse would be Jack Jones, getting ready to seduce me on top of the lobby's player piano.

"Come on, Elvis. Let's go. Please."

He gives me his daredevil look and swims to the other side of the fountain, sending the Peabody ducks into a frenzy of flapping and squawking and the duck master into near apoplexy. The crowd claps and presses closer to see what will happen next.

I already know. The Valentine contingent and our dog who thinks he's famous are going to be tossed out on our collective ear.

I'm no pushover: I resort to bribery. "Elvis! Pup-Peroni!" He makes a sharp turn, prances down the duck ramp and strolls nonchalantly in my direction. I wish everybody would stop laughing and clapping. It only encourages him.

Elvis shakes himself, wags his tail, and takes a few bows (I swear, that's what it looks like) before he lets me scoop him up. I try to blend into the crowd, but Lovie barges ahead of us, dripping water and wet wads of tissue all over the marble floor. She wouldn't try to blend even if she could.

Somewhere behind us a deep male voice booms, "What's going on here?"

"Quick, Lovie. The stairs." We duck (no pun intended) into the stairwell and hotfoot it to our room on the fourth floor. I slam the door shut behind us, then lean against it and listen for an irate person of importance to show up and demand explanations.

When somebody does pound on the door, I nearly have a heart attack. What if it's hotel security? What if they have a key?

I glance through the peephole and see the top of a head. Male. Longish hair slicked back.

"Ma'am?" The intruder hammers away at the door, then shifts so I can see his face, and I reach for the latch.

"Don't answer it," Lovie shouts, but I swing the door open.

"You forgot your shoes." It's the boys who rescued Lovie. The taller of the two holds out my Kate Spades.

"How did you know where to find me?"

"We followed you up the stairs."

Lovie's already rummaging around for a tip. A twenty-dollar one. From *my* purse.

After the boys leave I say, "Couldn't you have given them a smaller bribe?"

"I didn't want you to look cheap."

She glances at the clock and dives into the shower. It's only thirty minutes to show time and she's in this evening's tango competition. Lovie takes more time gilding her lily than any woman I know. It's going to take a major miracle to get her out the door on time.

Her dance partner (as well as Fayrene's) is Bobby Huckabee, Uncle Charlie's new assistant in the funeral home. Actually he's been with us since this summer's Elvis impersonator caper (as we now call it), but we still call him new.

It takes more than a few months to know the complicated Valentines, even if you do have a psychic eye. (Bobby has mismatched eyes and claims the blue one is psychic, though I've yet to see definitive proof.)

I'm still toweling Elvis dry when Lovie emerges from the shower. Without asking, I grab a hair dryer and start fluffing her hair while she jiggles into a green feathered and sequined costume. Feathers fly every which way.

"I look like a molting jungle parrot. Whoever picked out this costume?"

"You did. Hold still before I scorch your feathers."

She jiggles some more and fabric tears. The side slit intended to show a bit of leg becomes an open doorway to paradise. As if we weren't up to our necks in trouble already. I grab some safety pins and set to work.

"Just let it go, Callie. I want the judges to be so busy looking at me, they don't notice my partner can't dance worth a flitter."

Poor Bobby. I'm going to clap very loud for him.

With Elvis in pink bowtie and securely on his leash, we finally head to the Tennessee Exhibition Hall. Also known as Peabody Alley and directly connected to the hotel mezzanine, it has a huge ballroom on the second floor. The Memphis Ballroom is already teeming with dancers ranging in age from twenty to eighty-five.

The first dance is an open invitation, which means you can dance even if you didn't enter the competition.

Currently Elvis is behaving (meaning he's being petted and admired) but I'm not about to leave him for one minute, even if a nice-looking man named something-or-other Mims—I didn't quite catch his first name—is asking me to dance.

"Thank you, but no." The words are hardly out of my mouth before a pretty blond-haired woman drags him off. She's wearing a wedding ring, a pink dress, and red lipstick that clashes. He calls her *Babs honey* in a wheedling sort of way while she pouts. I wonder if she's his wife and how their marriage came to this.

I get a funny feeling up under my breastbone. They're about my age, and a terrible reminder that the fairy tale version of things can be dead wrong.

Fayrene, in a frilly green dress that makes her look like a head of romaine lettuce, joins me. Fortunately, I like salad. Though Mama says anything she wants, she taught me to always say nice things about people.

"That's a lovely shade of green, Fayrene."

"Thanks, Callie." Fayrene plops into the chair beside me. "I deflowered so much roast beef I thought I wasn't going to get it zipped."

Babs honey and her partner are dancing by and do a double take. I want to stop them and explain she meant *devoured* but I don't get a chance. The Mimses—if they are Mr. and Mrs.—will just have to spend the rest of the evening wondering about Fayrene's relationship to her rump roast.

"Are you entered in tonight's competition, Fay-rene?"

"No. I don't feel right doing Latin dances without Jarvetis. But do you think I can get him to budge? Oh no, he wants to stay down there sulking because I'm gone. Didn't even fix himself any lunch. Just sat there and ate Fruit of the Looms."

Thinking I'll have to clarify that she meant Fruit Loops, I look for the Mims couple, but they're on the other side of the floor.

The free dance ends, and twenty-five couples entered in the mambo competition take the floor. Mama and Mr. Whitenton are number twenty-two.

"There they are." Fayrene punches me as if I could look anywhere else.

Mama simply shines, and it's not merely from the gold dress. If I weren't so busy watching to see where Mr. Whitenton puts his hands, I'd be fascinated watching her dance. She's gyrating in body parts I didn't even know she had.

Sometimes I wish I could bottle Mama's spirit and put it on a shelf for inspiration. If I could filter out her penchant for trouble and tone down her sassy tongue, I'd want to be just like her.

After the mambo is over, she joins us. Mr. Whitenton is conspicuously absent, but I don't ask. I'm just grateful to have her to myself.

"Was I good?" Mama is like Elvis; she loves compliments, the more lavish the better.

"Fantastic," I tell her, and Fayrene says, "My ESPN tells me you're going to win."

ESP, I hope. But with Mama you never know. She could make headlines on the six o'clock news.

They link arms and head toward the outside hallway to get refreshments. I don't follow because Lovie and Bobby Huckabee have just taken the floor and I want to see their tango.

With the lights dancing all over her dress and her hair, Lovie looks like the goddess of some exotic island while poor Bobby looks like Ichabod Crane on the edge of hysteria. All he needs to push him over is the headless horseman.

If Jack were here, I'd send him to rescue Lovie's hapless partner. The music starts and I suddenly realize Elvis is missing.

Did Mama take him without telling me? That's not like her. I'm about to panic when my dog comes strolling back with telltale crumbs around his muzzle. As if sneaking around stealing cookies wasn't bad enough, he's eyeing the dance floor. The next thing I know he'll be out there doing the tango.

I nab him in the nick of time. "Behave yourself."

Bobby is off to a slow start and Lovie's doing her best to distract the judges. I didn't know she could kick her legs that high. If they go any higher, everybody in the audience will be seeing Christmas (my grandmother's term for private parts you have no business exposing to the public).

With all those whirling, sweating bodies, the room warms up and so does Bobby. By the time the tango ends he's downright loose.

He and Lovie come off the floor beaming.

"Let's celebrate," she says.

"With what?"

"Chocolate cherry cake."

"The reception starts in an hour," I tell her. "They'll have plenty of food."

"We'll get a head start. Besides, I want to get out of this dress. These feathers itch."

Bobby joins us in our room for cake, and when Lovie gets up to change, he says, "I'd better be going."

"Sit down, Bobby," she says. "I'm not going to do a striptease. Though I'm not above it."

His ears turn red. "I guess I'll have another piece. Of cake." He turns practically purple.

I feel sorry for him. While Lovie's in the bathroom changing, I cast around for topics that might capture his imagination and put his mind at ease. I'm not good at small talk and much prefer heart-to-hearts with good friends like Lovie.

"I notice *Phantom of the Opera* is playing at the Orpheum." That's Memphis' old Grand Opera House, used now for concerts and Broadway-type shows.

"There's danger," he says.

"Well, yes, I suppose you could call the phantom dangerous, but I see him more as a wounded musical genius."

"Danger from a dark-eyed stranger."

Bobby's looking off into space with his blue eye while the green one stares right at me. Though I know he has no powers to speak of, I get goose bumps. Fortunately, Lovie bursts back into the room, trailing black lace and White Shoulders perfume (her fragrance of choice).

"Let's go," she says, and I'm relieved to head up to the Skyway. It's a swing era supper club at the top of the Peabody, art deco styling, big polished dance floor, tables with white linen cloths behind a filigree railing that makes you think Bugsy Siegel is fixing to come in and sit down.

By the time we arrive, the competitive dancing couples are already there. Four hundred of them. In the crush, Bobby gets separated from us, which gives me a chance to shake off his dire prediction and quiz Lovie.

"Did I hear you on the phone while you were in the bathroom?"

"Yes. I called Rocky to tell him about my tango. Poor man."

"What do you mean, *poor man*?"

"To hear me tell it, I had every man in the ballroom salivating."

"What did he say?"

"I don't know. He was down in a Mayan burial ground or something, and we lost the connection."

The band plays "Stardust," and a tall, big-boned woman who could use some fashion and hair advice floats by with Bobby in tow. Her dress has more colors than Joseph's Technicolor Dreamcoat, and whoever did her hair ought to have his styling license revoked. I might sidle up later and hand her my card.

A few couples step onto the dance floor but most of them drift toward the Plantation Roof terrace where Lovie, Elvis, and I join them. The terrace is home of the duck palace, a glorified indoor–outdoor duck pen with the housing section built to look like a white-columned Southern mansion. Elvis perks up immediately and drags me in that direction.

I don't know whether he plans to terrorize the ducks or lord it over them that he stole their thunder in the fountain. Either way, I'm fixing to foil his plans. Probably with more bribery.

I wish I wouldn't be such a pushover.

I'm pulling a Milk-Bone out of my purse when the duck master starts flapping his hands at us.

"No dogs allowed!"

What does he think I am? Deaf? I don't know where the Peabody found this duck master— Melvin Galant, his nametag says—but I'm guessing the turnip patch. Of course, to be fair, if I had to go around all day wearing that silly-looking uniform with too much gold braid and the pants too short, I'd be surly, too.

Elvis threatens to lift his leg on the duck master's polished patent leather shoes, but I drag him back into the crowd before we get banned from Memphis. Though the duck master is probably no more than thirty-five, he looks like he hasn't smiled in fifteen years and would just as soon march you out in tar and feathers as look at you.

"Let's look at the river, Elvis."

Apparently everybody else has the same idea because we can't even get close to the ornate, Italian-style concrete balustrade. Still, the view of the Mississippi is magnificent.

"Isn't this peaceful?"

The words are no sooner out of my mouth than there's an explosion of flapping wings. Feathers fly, ducks squawk, and a high-pitched scream rips the air. Crowd control vanishes.

While I drag Elvis out of the melee, I glance around to see if I can locate the source of this near riot.

When I do, my stomach turns. I open my mouth to yell, but somebody beats me to it.

"It's Babs Mabry Mims!"

Not anymore. What's left of her is plastered on the sidewalk thirteen stories below.

Elvis' Opinion #2 on Lies, Limelight, and Duck Soup

There hasn't been this much excitement in Memphis since I started a musical revolution with "That's All Right."

Sirens blare and the cops arrive while feathers and tempers fly all over the place. Nearly everybody on the rooftop has a different story. Some swear they saw Babs jump while some vow she was drunk and fell, though how you'd accidentally fall over a substantial concrete parapet is a mystery to me.

They're all wrong. Babs Mabry Mims' death was neither an accident nor suicide. I know what I know. Something foul's afoot, and I'm not talking about the Peabody ducks.

If Callie would turn me loose, I'd find out a thing or two. In spite of my attempts to drag her toward the action, she's got me on a short leash.

Listen, if she thinks I'm going to apologize for getting in the Peabody fountain, she's barking up the wrong tree. I was putting on the best show this joint has seen since my heyday at Graceland. I didn't even get to finish my act. She's the one who ought to be apologizing.

As it is, I'm stuck with nothing but my radar ears.

What's this I hear?

Ruby Nell grabs ahold of a cop and jumps right in the middle of things.

"It was murder," she says.

"Back up, lady. I'm busy trying to contain this crowd."

You don't give Ruby Nell orders. Especially not in that tone of voice.

"She was pushed."

You can hear Ruby Nell all the way to the Mississippi River. This is a woman used to taking command. She draws the attention of another of Memphis' finest.

"Wait a minute, Bert," he says. "Let's hear what the lady has to say."

Bert hustles off while the second cop draws Ruby Nell aside. Determined to sleuth on the sly, I wiggle between the legs of a woman the size of a Toyota truck. If she decides to move, I'm sausage.

"Now, ma'am, why do you think Ms. Mims was pushed?" the cop asks Ruby Nell.

"Because somebody tried to push me off the roof, too. If I weren't so graceful and agile, I'd be lying down there on the sidewalk."

"Did you see who pushed you?"

"Of course not. If I had, he'd be walking around minus a few body parts."

The crowd laughs in the nervous way of people

horrified by what happened but grateful it happened to somebody else.

I get distracted by a ruckus over by the glorified duck pen everybody around here insists on calling a duck palace. *Duck palace*, my hind foot. You have to be royalty to live in a palace. Which, of course, I am. But what did I call my home? Graceland, which says it all.

Peering from under the skirts of Toyota Truck Lady, I glance at the duck pen to see what's going on. The duck master is trying to round up his infamous fowl, but they're too dumb to get back in their pen. They're flapping around the heads of three policemen who are trying to question a suspect.

He's none other than the guy who asked my human mom to dance earlier in the evening. And he has the look of a man on the hot seat.

Fortunately, I don't even have to leave my hiding place (and risk bodily injury in this melee) to see what's going on. I have a mismatched ear for trouble, and I've already caught this guy's act. He is H. Grayson Mims III—Babs Mabry Mims' current husband.

H. Grayson is twisting and turning in the wind because of Babs' first husband, Victor Mabry, who is also talking to the police and has their full attention.

"I tell you, Grayson Mims pushed her off the roof," the deposed first husband is shouting. "I saw him."

The crowd perks up and everybody looks surprised except the eyewitness and yours truly. Judging by the fracas I heard between H. Grayson,

Victor, and Babs earlier in the evening when I slipped my leash and sneaked out to find a little smackerel of something good, I'd say both husbands had plenty of motives to do her in. Extramarital shenanigans, if you believe the accusations they were hurling around.

I don't have enough evidence to convict either of them yet, but I'm hot on the trail and I have a plan. Being a dog of superior intelligence, I'm an expert planner.

Ask Trey. If it weren't for my masterly machinations, he'd be long gone from Mooreville. After that big fight Jarvetis and Fayrene had this summer over building a séance room at the back of Gas, Grits, and Guts, Jarvetis would have snatched him up and left the country. As it is, Trey is down on Ruby Nell's farm living off fat rabbits and the fat of the land while Jarvetis, unaware of his whereabouts, cools his heels. His bags are all packed, but he's not about to leave Fayrene without his favorite redbone hound.

Tonight after everything quiets down, I'll roust Callie out of bed so I can heed the call of nature. I can hold my bladder all night if I want to, but it has come in handy more than once when I wanted to get outside and mark a bush or two and howl at the moon.

What's the use of being in a hotel where one of my personal heroes (General Robert E. Lee) once roamed if I can't get out and sniff out his scent? Mess with me and I'm liable to even mark the spot.

While I'm taking care of business, I'll do a little doggie detection. And if I see any of those dumb ducks wandering about, tomorrow's menu will feature duck soup.

Toyota shifts and I come within a gnat's hair of biting her bulging ankle. *Listen lady, that's my tail you're stepping on*. I may have to take another dip in the fountain to get the kinks out.

Chapter 3

Messages, Mallards, and Gloria Divine

I'd be worried to death that somebody really did try to kill Mama if I didn't know she's a drama queen. Everybody in the Valentine family knows it. Just let some big event occur, and she jumps right into the middle of it.

If I don't get her off this roof I'm going to be up to my neck in murder again (a prospect I don't plan to repeat after this summer's fiasco with the Elvis impersonators).

I tug the leash and my dog appears from underneath the skirts of a woman who shouldn't be wearing horizontal red and white stripes. She looks like a circus tent.

See, I'm too upset to even think of anything nice to say like *She makes you long for pink cotton candy and Lipizzaner stallions in the center ring*.

"Come on, boy. Let's get Mama."

Lovie has already found her and is trying to talk some sense into her.

"You were probably just jostled, Aunt Ruby Nell."

"I know jostling from pushing. I was pushed."

Bobby Huckabee materializes. "There's danger all around you, Ruby Nell. Danger from a dark-eyed stranger." If I weren't such a lady, I'd say a word. One of Lovie's. Instead I content myself with giving him a scowl. But only a small one. He's so timid I don't want to scare him and hurt his feelings.

"Let's go downstairs, Mama. All of us could use a drink."

"Stop treating me like I'm senile. I know what happened and what didn't happen. And I'll leave when I'm good and ready."

Where's Fayrene when you need her? Right now I'd even be glad to see Mr. Whitenton. But he's still strangely absent. Personally, I think that's a good thing.

Unless he's waiting in Mama's room with a bottle of champagne and some bad intentions.

"Where's Mr. Whitenton?" I ask.

Mama narrows her eyes. "Why do you ask?"

Fayrene appears, saving me from thinking up a lie. Though I'm not above an occasional prevarication, I don't like it, even if it's just a little white one.

"I could use a shot of Wild Turkey." Fayrene puts her hand over her heart. "Somebody nearly pushed me off the roof."

Mama shoots me this *See, I told you* look.

"Let's all go to Mallards," I say.

It's a charming pub in the Peabody, and frankly I'll be glad to get away from tonight's uncivilized business. If you are of weak character (which I definitely am not), this kind of evening could make you take up civilized drinking.

I head toward the elevator and, thank goodness, they all pile in behind me. I punch the button for the lobby.

"Wait for me in the pub," I tell them. "I have to take Elvis outside, and then put him in the room."

Even if my basset does have special permission to be in the hotel, I don't think that extends to the restaurants. After the incident in the fountain, I'm not about to call attention to him again.

Though I'd love to pass unnoticed through the Grand Lobby, Elvis has other ideas. He preens and prances and shakes his ample self every which way. He draws a crowd as easily as the King. Children and adults alike surround us, asking if they can pet him.

Sometimes I actually believe my dog is a reincarnation of the singer Bruce Springsteen called his *religion*. If this kind of public adoration keeps up, I can forget hiring a manicurist. I'm going to have to hire a bodyguard. For my dog.

Fortunately my cell phone rings, and the crowd disperses to give me some privacy. Unfortunately, it's Jack.

"Where are you?" I ask. With his mysterious Company fresh on my mind, I want to know. No. I'm desperate to know.

"Changing planes."

"Where?"

"A long way from home."

"We don't have a home, Jack."

I hear nothing but long-distance static and the

scream of silence. I'm getting ready to hang up when he says, "Cal?"

There's longing in his voice, nostalgia for those sweet moments on the porch swing where the scent of jasmine hung heavy on the air and our future was an endless, shining road. My grip on the phone tightens and so does my throat.

What's he going to say? *I'm sorry? Let's start over?*

I hang on to Elvis' leash, my heart full of hope.

"Be careful in Memphis."

Vain hope, it turns out. I should have known better. I know Jack. I know him well.

"I wish you'd stop keeping tabs on my whereabouts."

"I will always know where you are, Cal."

That's it. Nothing more. Just the huge silence of a broken connection.

I burst through the doors of the Peabody and suck in the sultry night air. Wouldn't you know? A horse-drawn wedding carriage sits under the maroon Peabody Hotel canopy appliquéd with white ducks, the bride and groom in a huddle on the high leather seat.

I want to rush up, grab them by the coattails and say, "Wait." Just that. Wait.

Instead I rush into the dusk with Elvis, who makes a beeline for the red and green caladiums. I drag him away from the flowerbeds and into the parking lot where he lifts his leg on a tire. A Cadillac, naturally. Except it's not pink.

I can't face my family right now. Mama would see right through me, ply me with questions. I take off down the sidewalk in a fast trot. With the crowds coming out for a night of barbecued ribs and gut-bucket blues, I can't take the kind of run I do back home in my own neighborhood, but it's enough to clear my head.

When Elvis and I get back to the room, the message light is blinking, but the front desk says there's a telegram for Lovie. I'm glad it's not for me. Really. With Jack off heaven knows where doing no telling what, I can do without the suspense of getting a telegram.

It would be just like Jack Jones to be up to his neck in deep-cover skullduggery. He could have already been shot in the airport, for all I know.

The Company sounds clandestine to me. When I get home I'm going to ask Uncle Charlie. The two of them are thick. He'll know.

Whether he'll tell me is another matter. He's the kind of man who keeps secrets and makes you think it's for your own good.

"If you could talk, I'll bet you'd tell me what Jack does, wouldn't you, boy?"

Elvis comes over to be petted and then I get his guitar-shaped pillow out of the suitcase. I'd never make him sleep on the floor, even if it does have carpeting.

I'm just getting him settled beside my bed when my cell phone rings. It's Champ, saying he's planning to drive to Memphis tomorrow to *see about me*.

That's the last thing I need—a man who wants to hover around protecting me. As far as I can tell, Champ's overprotective attitude is his only fault. Jack may break and enter and do all manner of wicked things, but he understands my need for independence.

Of course, he bends the truth to suit himself, while Champ would never do such a thing.

See, that's what I mean about needing a relaxing weekend. All this comparative thinking is giving me a headache.

"I'm fine, Champ. Really. Everything's fine."

Aside from a little murder and Elvis' caper in the fountain and Bobby's depressing predictions and Mr. Whitenton's connecting door and Jack's disturbing phone call. I wish I'd wake up in my own bed and discover all this was a bad dream.

"Are you sure, Callie? Your voice sounds strained."

"It's been a long day." I tell him about the dance competition so I won't sound abrupt and hurt his feelings.

"Sounds like fun. Are you sure you don't want me to come?"

"Positive. 'Night, Champ."

Elvis gives me this look, and I'd swear he heard both ends of the conversation and understood every word.

"Don't look at me like that. At least Champ asks, which is more than Jack does. He just barges around doing whatever he pleases."

Some people might feel silly talking to a dog, but I don't. I believe every living thing on this earth is interconnected, and I treat my dogs and cats with courtesy and kindness. Even my philodendrons.

Everybody is waiting for me in Mallards. Lovie pushes a big strawberry daiquiri my way. She knows me well.

While Fayrene holds forth on her *narrow escape from the grim reaper* (her words, not mine), I tell Lovie about the telegram.

"Who from?"

"I didn't ask. It's for you, not me."

Mama and Bobby are too busy listening to Fayrene to hear our exchange.

"If it hadn't been for the sirens," she's saying, "I'd be dead. I was just about to tip over the edge of the roof when they started wailing and whoever wanted me to die ran off. I tell you, it was divine invention."

I could use a little of that myself, both intervention and invention. If I want to spend my evening talking about something besides murder, I'm going to have to think of a clever way to steer the conversation elsewhere.

"Bobby, who was that very attractive woman you were with earlier?" I ask.

"Gloria Divine. She's a peach."

"Her face looked familiar," Mama says. "What does she do?"

"She didn't say."

"You mean she just picked you up and you don't know a thing about her?" Mama can get by with asking Bobby questions like that. He thinks she and Fayrene walk on water, mainly because they believe in his psychic eye. To be fair, though, he's also captivated by their joie de vivre, especially Mama's. She always has that effect on people.

"She has an uncle with uneven eyes," Bobby says. "She recognized my abilities right off."

"I've been married to Jarvetis forty years and he still hasn't recognized my abilities." Fayrene slugs back her Vodka Collins. "Don't get me started. My acid reflex will start acting up."

"How old was she, Bobby?" Mama is shameless. "I'm all for older women with younger men, but she looked a little long in the tooth for you."

Fayrene nods. "She looked like she'd had a face lift to me. Probably breast entrancement surgery, too."

Acid reflex was bad enough, but breast entrancement nearly cracks me up. Lovie's about to lose it, too. She kicks me under the table, a signal we developed in high school when one of us wanted to escape and needed the other to provide a good excuse.

"Lovie, I need to check on Elvis. You want to go up with me?"

I tell Mama to put the tab on my room. Listen, I know my soft-touch ways are dragging me toward the brink of financial ruin, but I'm too busy trying to untangle my messy marital status to attempt a major self-improvement course. My goal is to change myself into a woman of means and resolve before I'm forty, so I still have three years. Of course, my most pressing goal is to start a family before then, but the way things are going, my eggs will be atrophied before I ever get the chance.

As soon as we're out of earshot, Lovie says, "Maybe there is something to Aunt Ruby Nell's and Fayrene's stories about being pushed."

"I doubt it, and I'm not fixing to borrow that trouble." I punch the elevator button harder than I have to, and we get in.

"But Callie, don't you think it's odd that Grayson Mims' accuser was Victor Mabry?"

"I'm certainly not going to get in the middle of that."

"Both have been her husbands. That's suspicious."

"Let it alone, Lovie."

"I can't help it if I have a talent for detective work."

"What you have is a talent for trouble."

The door slides open and she flounces out. I'm not a natural like her, but I can flounce, too. It hampers my progress but I soon catch up.

"Listen, Lovie, if you really want a girls' weekend out, you'll hush up about finding the killer. Unless you actually like breaking the law."

With her, you never know. After all, she did date Slick Fingers Johnson, who, according to her, knew his way around locks as well as he did the Holy Grail.

"If we hadn't broken the law, I'd never have met Rocky."

I can't argue there. He would never have followed us to Tupelo if we hadn't broken and entered out in Las Vegas (during what the Valentine family now refers to as the Bubbles Caper).

I slide the key into the lock. "Still, that does not mean I'm going to don a disguise and nose around. For goodness sake, Lovie, this is the *Peabody*."

You might as well say the name in the same breath as the Deep South. Historians say the Mississippi Delta begins in the lobby of the Peabody and ends on Catfish Row in Vicksburg, Mississippi. If you stand by the fountain long enough, they say you'll see everybody who is anybody.

Not that I'm planning to stand by the fountain. After Elvis' shenanigans, I don't plan to get near that place again. All I want is to climb into bed and get a good night's sleep.

While Lovie calls the front desk for her message, I put on my Betty Boop pajamas and head to the bathroom to brush my teeth. When I emerge she says, "The telegram was from Rocky, wishing me good luck in the competition."

"He's a sweet man. Now can I go to sleep?"

"Just because he's sweet doesn't mean I'm not planning to put a burr under his saddle."

"You've already done that. I think he's immune to burrs."

"Wait till he hears what I plan to do with the jitterbug."

"Don't tell me. I don't want to know." I've had all the drama I can stand for one day. I roll my back toward her and pull the sheet over my head.

Chapter 4

Horse-drawn Carriages, the Peabody Fountain, and Something Fishy

Somebody is tugging my sheet. If it's Lovie I'm going to kill her.

"What? What!" I bolt upright, bleary eyed. Lovie is snoring on the other bed, but my dog is dancing around by mine with the edge of my sheet between his teeth. "Good grief, Elvis. Not now."

Groaning, I lie back down, but I might as well be trying to sleep on the deck of a rolling ship. I don't know how a basset hound, even a portly one, can shake a whole bed along with its hundred-twenty-pound occupant. I guess it's something about the way he leans against the mattress and proceeds to rub his back.

"Stop that. I'm coming."

I pull on sweats but add my cute Coach Dawnell Patchwork sneakers (I'm not about to take up un-stylish shoe habits, even if it is 3 A.M.). Then I grab his leash and stumble out into the empty hallway.

"You're going to owe me for this, boy."

This time of night the elevator gives me the creeps. Elvis and I get in, and I scoot to the corner and keep my back against the wall. When it stops on the second floor I panic. Nobody is out this time of night. Unless they happen to be doggie mom to Elvis.

Tomorrow's headline in the Memphis *Commercial Appeal* will read, "Mississippi Hair Stylist and Her Dog, the King, Die Mysterious Death in Elevator."

The only weapon I have is my dog, and though he growls a good show, I don't know how effective he'd be against a Peabody killer stalking his prey in the middle of the night.

When the door slides open I brace myself to see a suspicious-looking person waiting on the other side. Thank goodness, nobody's there. I let out the breath I've been holding.

Finally the door slides shut again and we swoosh downward. Did I push two buttons? Or was the murderer out there looking for another victim, then at the last minute changed his mind?

I can't get out of this elevator fast enough. When we reach the lobby, I bolt. Elvis has other ideas. Marking the elevator, for one thing.

"No, you don't." I tug him out in the nick of time. "Hurry, boy. Outside."

He gives me his stubborn look and tries to drag me toward the fountain. You wouldn't think a dog his size could drag a woman mine, but you don't know Elvis. When he makes up his mind, he's like his namesake. Not much can stop him.

Promises of Milk-Bone and Pup-Peroni usually

do the trick. Unfortunately I don't have any doggie treats on me. Call me a wimpy pushover, but when it comes to Elvis, I'm not too proud to beg and plead.

"Listen, Elvis. If you'll behave I'll personally take you to see Ann-Margret and the pups when we get home."

That does the trick. Who'd ever have believed my opinionated, self-centered basset hound would take to the role of fatherhood? Who wouldn't love them, though? Three darling French poodle-basset hound mixes and two who look suspiciously like the shih tzu down the street. Only don't mention that to Elvis. He hasn't noticed yet.

Outside, Union Avenue is practically empty. While Elvis is sniffing every inch of the sidewalk, headlights cut through the gloom and a cab pulls up from the direction of the river to deposit Mr. Whitenton, of all people.

Though it's not that cold, he's wearing an overcoat with the collar pulled high around his neck and a felt hat circa 1942 pulled low over his eyes. Thank goodness Mama is not with him.

It's hard to miss a sassy basset hound sniffing a fire hydrant right in front of your nose, but Thomas acts like he doesn't see us. Suspicious behavior if I ever saw it.

What's he doing out so late? And why is he dressed like Clifton Young in *Dark Passage*? I can imagine Mr. Whitenton saying, *I was a small time crook until this very minute, and now I'm a big time crook.*

"Mr. Whitenton," I call out, but he scuttles off like somebody's following him and he's about to lose his head.

Where was he when Babs was murdered? In disguise pushing her off the roof?

I'd follow him—if nothing else but to make sure he doesn't go into Mama's room—but Elvis has yet to select a place for his business. While he's sniffing the curb, a horse-drawn carriage with a weary-looking driver stops in front of the hotel. Who should climb down but Victor Mabry, Babs Mabry Mims' husband number one.

The woman with him is wearing a ring, and I assume it's the second Mrs. Mabry. She looks young enough to have a curfew and parents waiting up worrying about her. She's much younger than he, the cheerleader type, cute, petite, blond, and bubbly. That alone is suspicious. Nobody bubbles at the crack of dawn except teenagers and fish.

They wave at Elvis and me, moderating my suspicions, but not entirely, then go into the hotel with their arms wrapped around each other. I'm stabbed by a feeling I'd like to call nostalgia, but to tell the truth, I think it's jealousy. I swear if I had somebody wonderful to put his arms around me on a committed full-time basis, I'd give up designer shoes. At least the more expensive ones.

I stamp around on the sidewalk and beat my arms. "Hurry up, Elvis. It's chilly out." I'm beginning to think he just wanted to get out of the hotel.

Finally he deigns to pee and we head back inside. I go for the bank of elevators, but Elvis is pulling so hard on the leash I'm dragged along in the opposite direction. I dig in my heels, but skid across the marble floors straight toward the fountain.

I could pull hard enough to stop him, but I'm not about to choke my dog. Finally I give up and barrel along in his wake.

The cherubs on the fountain smile as we approach. They're sitting atop ancient dolphins that in my opinion look more like fish. Each cherub has one arm uplifted, holding aloft a giant urn filled with stargazer lilies.

Jack and I had stargazer lilies at our wedding. The fragrance makes me dizzy. Or maybe it's the memories. Or it could be the ungodly hour. Nobody's out this time of night unless they're holding a dog leash or up to no good.

The closer I get, the dizzier I feel. Something's not right. I feel it in my bones.

And then I see the Technicolor dress. And the bad hairdo.

Gloria Divine is lying face down in the water.

"Help!" I kick off my shoes. "Over here! In the fountain!"

I leap into the fountain and tug Gloria. Water-logged bodies are heavier than you'd think.

"I need some help!"

If I can get her out of the fountain I might revive her. The cell phone in my pocket rings. I'm up to my knees in water and have my hands full to boot. I can't worry about who's calling this time of night.

"Hey, lady! What are you doing?" The night manager is looming over me wearing a badge, a shocked look, and too much hair gel.

"I'm trying to get her out."

And why isn't he helping? Gloria Divine weighs as much as a side of beef (no disrespect intended). I'm slender (Lovie calls me *skinny*), but fortunately I work out enough to have more upper body strength than you'd think.

Taking a deep breath, I heave the top half of Gloria Divine over the edge of the travertine marble. Mr. No-help-at-all whips out his cell phone and calls the police. Ignoring him, I struggle with the bottom half of Gloria.

"Are you crazy?" He snaps his phone shut. "Put her back."

"I know CPR."

"She's dead."

"What if she's not?"

I can't believe I'm having this conversation. Then it hits me: Gloria Divine is blue and stiff. That means she's dead (unless I'm fixing to witness a resurrection), and I'll be caught red-handed trying to move the body.

Sirens shrill this way, and sleepy guests roused from their beds straggle into the lobby in pajamas and jeans with their shirttails hanging out. I try to climb from the fountain (unsuccessfully, might I add), but nobody helps me. They're glued to the floor like people seeing an ungodly apparition.

Elvis is the only one offering encouragement. He's sitting there like a gentleman, his tail thumping the floor.

My feet slip on something gooey (I don't even want to know) and I end up hanging on to a pair of icy cold legs. A dead woman's legs.

What was I thinking? For a woman who spent all

day trying to keep her distance from murder, I've landed smack dab in the middle of it.

As if things couldn't get any worse, the cops are barreling my way. They see me with the body and jerk their guns out of their holsters.

Holy cow. I'm going to end up shot in the fountain. Probably in the head, too.

Chapter 5

Dancing Bodies, Wacky Witnesses, and Pepto-Bismol

"Don't move. Hands in the air, lady."

I wish everybody would quit calling me "lady." "I found her like this."

It's hard to talk when you're slipping and sliding in duck gunk and your hands are over your head. Besides, I'm wet up to my thighs and shaking with chill.

Why doesn't the night manager speak up? Ken Peacock, his badge reads. Is everything fowl in this hotel?

"I was trying to save her. Ask him."

Thankfully a seasoned-looking cop pulls Peacock aside, and I hear the night manager say he didn't see or hear a thing until I yelled for help. A fresh-faced freckled cop helps me from the fountain, and somebody throws a blanket over my shoulders.

The young cop takes my name and asks what I was doing out at this time of night.

"Elvis had to take care of business."

He looks at me like I've gone crazy. I have tennis shoes older than this cop. No wonder he doesn't understand how people are still naming their dogs and cats and birds and babies after a man who has been dead more than thirty-five years. Listen, Elvis not only changed the face of music but is still beloved the world around.

"He's a basset hound," I explain.

"Not in this town, lady." Unsmiling, he jots something in his notebook. Probably, *Get the net*.

Leave it to me to get a cop without a sense of humor. If it weren't for the bit of powdered sugar on his shirt, I'd think he wasn't even human. He was probably having doughnuts and coffee when he got the call.

"Where's the dog?"

Good grief. In all the commotion, Elvis has disappeared. I clap my hands and try to whistle, but it comes out more of a squeak. "Here, boy, come here, Elvis." He's nowhere in sight.

"I thought you had a dog, lady."

"I do."

"Maybe he's not Elvis. Maybe he's Houdini."

Ignoring that crack, I whistle and call some more. When Elvis finally pokes his cold nose between my legs, I scoop him up and hide my face in his fur so this young cop won't see how close I am to tears.

Always attuned to my moods, Elvis turns on the charm. Which is considerable, might I add.

At last I get lucky. This boyish cop is a dog lover. He scratches Elvis' ears while he asks me if I knew the deceased. By the time I tell him about seeing Gloria only briefly on the rooftop and he tells me not to leave town, I'm getting a motherly urge to reach over and brush the sugar off his shirt.

Still, I know this score only too well. I'm on the list now. A witness and possibly a suspect.

For somebody who wanted to avoid murder at all costs, I'm smack dab in the middle of it.

A team from the coroner's office rushes by with the gurney, making this nightmare all too real. I'd like to go to my room and pretend all this has nothing to do with me, but I'm trapped now. I might as well learn what I can.

Keeping Elvis on a short leash and trying to be inconspicuous, I weave through the crowd. Though how I can remain anonymous looking like a rag mop fresh from a dirty kitchen floor, I have no idea. Not to mention the fact that everybody saw the cops grilling me.

Maybe if I slump . . . I ease as close as I dare to a middle-age woman claiming to be a witness. She's wearing a beige housecoat that washes out her complexion. Somebody ought to steer her toward pink.

"I registered the dancers," she's telling the cops. I remember her now. She was wearing red lipstick, a much more flattering color for her type. "Gloria Divine was entered in the waltz competition."

"What do you know about her, ma'am?" Though this cop looks no more than fifty, he's asking questions with the jaded attitude of a man who has been in this business too long and seen too much.

"She's from Tennessee. Nashville to be exact. She was in room 1014, right next to poor Babs Mabry Mims."

"Did they know each other?"

"Maybe. Maybe not. We reserved a block of rooms on the tenth floor. Most of the dancers are there. A few spilled over to the fourth."

I can tell the woman standing next to them is itching to butt in. She's about seventy and wearing a hairnet over pink foam rollers I wouldn't be caught dead in.

"That Gloria Divine's a mysterious woman," she chimes in. "Comes to all the dance competitions with a silver-haired partner. But I've never seen her with anybody else except a woman with a strange name—Lalique or something—and a funny-looking man with one blue eye and one green."

Holy cow. They're going to drag Bobby into this. Should I warn him or keep quiet so he won't worry? I think I'll opt for the latter. No use borrowing trouble before it arrives.

These two women don't offer anything else, so I move on toward another woman talking to the cops. She looks familiar from the back, but I'm too rattled to place her.

"Gloria Divine was one of the last to leave the Skyway," she's saying. "Around midnight."

I edge around the player piano to get a closer look. Lo and behold, this witness is the perky companion of Victor Mabry. Victor is hanging on to her like she's the kewpie doll prize he won at the county fair.

Personally, I don't trust a man who's that possessive. Did he feel the same way about his first wife? Would losing her make him mad enough to kill her?

"Drinking heavily," Victor confirms. "I saw her

have at least five drinks in the Skyway, and the waiter delivered a sixth while we were there. Obviously she got drunk and fell in."

How would he know? And why is he offering statements to the police on both murders?

"Was Gloria Divine alive when you last saw her?"

The cop's question causes Victor to look uncomfortable. I'm straining to hear, so I try to maneuver closer, but Elvis' leash gets tangled in a chair. It crashes to the floor just as my cell phone rings.

I might as well be in the center ring at a Barnum and Bailey circus. Conversation ceases and every head swivels in my direction. I scoop Elvis up, stick out my chin, and march out of the lobby. It's hard to make a dignified exit when your shoes are leaving duck-doo tracks and your cell phone is playing a raucous electronic version of the "William Tell Overture."

As soon as I round a marble column, I cast dignity to the winds and dash toward the elevators. Getting my cell phone out of my pocket while running with an armful of wiggling dog is not my idea of a fun-filled weekend.

"What?" I yell into the receiver.

"I've been attacked! In my bed! Somebody tried to kill me!"

I punch the tenth floor button and head straight to Mama's room.

It looks like Logan International. People and suitcases are everywhere. (Mama always travels with enough gear to go on an African safari.) Lovie is pressing a cloth to Mama's head, Fayrene is rubbing her feet, Thomas is urging her to take some Pepto-Bismol for her "upset" and Bobby is passing around breath mints.

For what, I don't know. Maybe they've all been drinking heavily and don't want me to know. I know. *I know.* I'm getting punchy. But considering the kind of night it has been, anything is possible

Thomas has changed from the film noir clothes I saw him wearing earlier to pajamas and robe. This man works fast. The bed clothes transform him from villain to scrawny man who wouldn't say boo if a panther had him by the seven hairs on his head and was dragging him off into the night. I don't trust a man who can alter his appearance that drastically.

"At last." Mama holds her arms out to me. "There you are."

For somebody who has just been attacked, she sounds mighty perky. Of course, what would you expect? Nothing intimidates her.

Hurrying over, I squat beside her bed and inspect her from head to toe. While I'm at it, I take a closer look at Thomas. His eyes are bloodshot and he looks nervous.

"Are you all right, Mama?"

"I will be as soon as everybody *quits hovering.*"

Don't let Mama fool you. She loves to be the object of outrageous displays of devotion, and everybody who loves her knows it. Nobody leaves their coveted spot beside the reigning queen.

"Where have you been?" She gives me the once over. "And what's that on your pants?"

"It's water and duck stuff. I was out walking Elvis and found Gloria Divine in the fountain."

Everybody in the room starts asking questions

except Thomas. Did he not hear? Or did he already know?

"Is she okay?" Mama asks.

"No. I tried to save her, but it was too late."

Bobby makes the sign of the cross in the air over Mama's bed. "There's danger everywhere."

Fayrene stops rubbing Mama's feet and strikes a dramatic pose. Washington crossing the Delaware.

"This business is starting to irrigate me."

I'm already *irrigated* and I'd be irritated, too, but I have bigger things on my mind.

"Mama, have you reported the attack?"

"No. I was waiting for you to get here."

I nod at Lovie, who calls the cops.

This kind of role reversal is not new. Mama bulldozes along telling folks what to do and doing as she pleases until there's a real crisis, then she relies on me to take charge.

While I'm assuring myself Mama is okay, Fayrene climbs into the other side of the bed and pulls up the covers.

"Wild hogs couldn't drag me out of here tonight, and don't you argue, Ruby Nell."

Mama doesn't. For one thing, the night's almost over.

"What happened up here?" I ask.

"I heard the commotion in Miss Ruby's room," Thomas bursts in before Mama can answer. "Of course, I rushed right to her aid."

Through the connecting door, obviously, which was unlocked and is standing wide open. Did Mama do that, or did he?

I make a mental note to get to the bottom of the unlocked connecting door.

"I was scratching and clawing and kicking like a wildcat." Mama sounds proud of herself. "I knocked the phone off and kicked my suitcase off the rack at the end of the bed."

"The minute I walked in, whoever was trying to kill Miss Ruby ran out."

"What did he look like?" I ask.

"It was a she," Thomas says. "Medium height. Black pants. Or it could have been blue jeans. Longish hair. Black."

"I don't think so, Thomas," Mama says, and he recants.

"Wait a minute. Her hair could have been red."

"Are you sure it was a woman?" I sound like the young cop, second guessing everybody. All I need is sugar on my sweats.

"It was definitely a woman." Thomas rams his hands into his pockets and rocks back and forth. "On second thought, it might have been a man. I saw it all and will testify to the fact."

"Mama? Was your attacker male or female?"

"Male. No doubt about it. When he tried to smother me with my pillow, I smelled his after-shave. Old Spice. No woman in her right mind would wear Old Spice."

Lovie catches my eye and nods toward Thomas, who is rubbing his chin. What I see gives me chills. If it weren't for my level head, I'd probably accuse him on the spot.

"Mr. Whitenton, you'd better put something on those scratches on your hands." I'm proud of my even tone. Only Lovie knows I'm barely holding myself together. "How'd you get them?"

"Oh. These?" He sticks his hands in his bath-robe pockets. "The attacker must have scratched me in the scuffle."

"What scuffle?"

Why didn't he mention it before? Was he lying when he said the attacker ran out when he walked in. Or is he lying now? I don't ask for fear of putting him on the defensive. You learn more if people think you trust them.

"There was so much commotion going on, I guess I forgot."

"I should call Daddy," Lovie says.

"Don't you dare call Charlie." Mama practically leaps out of the bed. "The day I need somebody keeping tabs on me is the day you can put me in a nursing home."

Mama's performance is interrupted by the ar-rival of the police. Unfortunately it's the sugar coated baby cop, and his tough as nails partner, who want to know what I'm doing at the scene of another attack.

They look skeptical when I explain, but I'm not about to be intimidated. I stick around for their questions. Unfortunately, I don't learn a new thing.

It's nearly dawn when Lovie and I leave, and my stomach is starting to rumble.

"I can't sleep," I tell Lovie. "Let's get out of this hotel. Someplace quiet. Besides, Elvis needs some real exercise."

"The river," she says.

I don't even take time to change clothes. They're almost dry and who's going to see me anyway? We grab a bag of his dog food, some doughnuts from Lovie's stash, and coffee made in the room, then head to the riverside park.

In the damp chill of dawn, we sit on benches with the rising sun at our backs, loading up on carbs and sugar. The play of color and light across the water is spectacular. Of one accord (Lovie and I can practically read each other's mind), we don't talk. Awe leaves no room for murder.

Until today "the mighty Mississippi" was merely a term I've heard since grade school. Now it's a visceral feeling, a bone-deep affirmation.

"It makes you feel like you ought to sing," Lovie says.

Why not? Maybe it will bring some sanity into chaos. Lovie and I sing duets at Wildwood Chapel all the time. When I start "How Great Thou Art" in a clear, high soprano, she joins in with a dusky-voiced alto.

Naturally Elvis prances up, throws back his head, and howls. It was one of his alter ego's biggest hits and his favorite song, to boot.

But music can't compete with murder, and the song peters out. My dog trots off to pee on an oak tree, and I start putting two and two together.

"I think Mr. Whitenton might have killed Gloria Divine," I tell Lovie. "And maybe even Babs Mabry Mims."

"What makes you think that? The scratches?"

"That, plus his early-morning taxi ride." I tell her about seeing him outside the hotel.

"But what was his motive? I think Babs' husband is the likeliest suspect."

"Which one? The first one or the second one?"

"The current. H. Grayson Mims."

"We have two dead bodies that are totally unrelated, Lovie. We need to broaden our investigation beyond next of kin. Besides, what else was Mr. Whitenton doing out at that time of night?"

"Catting around?"

"Get serious. At his age?"

"Let's hope so. If 'geriatric' means 'dead libido,' I'm not planning to celebrate another birthday after fifty."

She probably won't, either. I look around to see if my dog is staying out of trouble. He's over by a magnolia tree digging a hole.

"Did you notice Mr. Whitenton's aftershave?" I ask.

"It was very faint. I think it was English Leather. But even if it was Old Spice, why would he attack Aunt Ruby Nell?"

"I don't know, but anybody as colorful as Mama is bound to have given dozens of people multiple reasons to do her in. I just want to catch the killer before he makes Mama his next victim."

"Does this mean I get to wear a disguise?"

"No disguises, Lovie. And no clambering around in high places."

Who can forget Lovie in feathers mooning half of Las Vegas in what we now refer to as the Bubbles Caper? Us teetering on a rickety balcony in a monsoon as we tried to find out who was killing Elvis impersonators? And don't get me started on the hot air balloon.

"Agreed?"

"Of course not." Lovie stands up and dusts the powdered sugar off her pink tee shirt. You'd think the color would clash with her hair, but on her it looks great. "What's the use of doing anything if you can't have fun?"

Elvis' Opinion #3 on Big Secrets, Shady Pasts, and Back Alley Leftovers

This is what happens when you're the hottest, biggest box office star the world has ever seen and you die and get sent back in a dog suit: nobody asks your opinion about anything anymore. I once had minions hanging on my every word. One and a half billion people saw my telecast from Hawaii, and reporters were lined around the block to talk to me. Now I can't even get one person (my human mom, to be exact) to ask me what I know about Gloria Divine.

A lot, that's what. Of course, it was in my other life. I had a close business connection to her after I got back from Germany.

For your information, I'm a patriotic dog. I'd have joined the army anyway if they hadn't drafted me. I remember it well: 1958. The year after I bought Graceland.

I've had dealings behind closed doors with Gloria's girlfriend, too. *Lalique*, my mismatched ears. Her name is Latoya LaBelle, and she's a luscious fifty-nine and holding. Gloria was sixty-two and still stacked.

And that's all I'm saying on the subject. Listen, I may be a dog of character, but I've got a few skeletons rattling around in my past just like anybody else. The difference between me and the general public (besides talent and looks, of course) is that I know how to keep my mouth shut.

Bless'a my soul, what's this I see? A genuine American sternwheel steamboat cruising down the river. I sidle closer to the water to get a better look.

It's the Mississippi Queen, newly refurbished, I've heard, and looking like a riverboat gambler might step onto the deck at any minute. If I could get Ann-Margret and the pups up here, we'd take a family vacation on the river.

I've always wanted to go on a sternwheeler.

Back when I was starring in one movie after the other out in Hollywood, the Delta Queen still reigned. I used to hole up in the Knickerbocker Hotel and dream of ways I could get out of the glare of fame long enough to board that grand old lady (now retired) and cruise from Memphis down to New Orleans.

But no matter what disguise I thought up, my fans still recognized me. I couldn't go anywhere without causing a riot. I can still cause riots, but that's a whole 'nother story—and the price of fame.

Now all I'm trying to do is sneak down to the water's edge and give the tourists a thrill without Callie noticing. I trot toward a massive magnolia tree and when she looks up to check on me I pretend to be digging a hole.

Satisfied, she gets back to planning a murder investigation with Lovie. I dart behind the trunk and perk up my radar ears to see if the coast is still clear. It is, so I hotfoot it toward the river.

"Elvis! Come back here. You'll fall in the water."

Foiled. What does she think? I can't swim?

Still, I don't like to worry her so I waltz my ample backside up the bank, but I take my time about it. Next, I sit at her feet looking cute and perky so she'll scratch my ears.

Listen, you have to work these humans. You should never let them think they have the upper hand. That means you don't come directly when they call and you don't show remorse over anything, even if they catch you red-pawed.

If I sit here long enough, maybe Callie will bring me into the investigation. But *no*, she just keeps on acting like she and Lovie will do it all.

What does my human mom think I was doing in the hotel lobby this morning? Whistling "Don't Be Cruel?" I was sniffing out clues. Callie thinks she learned a lot when she overheard the police questioning Victor and Jill Mabry. (Listen, she doesn't even know Victor's wife's name.) If I told her what I know, she'd probably take me to the alley across Union and reward me with a little smackerel of pork barbecue from the Rendezvous.

You talk about great Southern cooking—I'd hold their ribs right up there with the ones we had at Graceland. The only difference is the Rendezvous uses a dry sauce and ours were wet. Of course, ribs don't compare with fried peanut butter and banana sandwiches, but I'm just a country dog at heart. Always have been, always will be.

But back to murder. . . . The second Mrs. Victor Mabry was spitting fire when I overheard her, and all because Victor said he was devastated over Babs' death. Let me tell you, she was mad enough to have killed Babs herself.

If you want my opinion, Jill Mabry is capable of having killed Gloria, too, but I've yet to sniff out their connection.

I'm being hustled off the riverbank now, but I have a plan. As soon as we get back to the Peabody, I'll start working all the angles of this murder. And while I'm at it, I'll be trying to find an escape hatch. The security is so tight around me you'd think I was wearing a spangled jumpsuit and still making a news headline like the one in 1974 that proclaimed, "Elvis for President."

I've got to find a way to slip out so I can pay homage to my fans at Graceland.

Elvis' Recipe for Wet Barbecue Sauce

First wag your tail and sidle up to Callie, humming "Stuck on You." If she doesn't succumb to flattery, paw the cabinet door open and knock over the tomato sauce and the chili powder.

Next, offer to squeeze the lemons to show you're helpful (indispensable, too, but she already knows that). She'll decline, of course. My human mom is something of a control freak. One of the things I have to teach her is how to let go. Relax. Forget the details and enjoy the big picture.

By now she's in the swing of lip-smacking good Southern ribs. Sit back, layer it on thick with a few bars of "Earth Angel" while she shakes, rattles, and rolls with red pepper, vinegar, pickling spice, and dried mustard.

Segue into "Sweet Sweet Spirit," a little reminder to dump in honey and brown sugar. Keep singing while she coats the ribs and socks them in the oven.

Bless'a my soul, the smell alone is enough to send you dancing through the doggie door in search of a spot to bury the bones. Gnawing the meat off first is optional. Personally, I'm partial to a bit of Mississippi red clay on my cuisine.

Chapter 6

Wild Goose Chase, Gibson Guitars, and Mojo Hands

As we hurry back to the hotel, I try not to think what I'm getting myself into. I try not to dwell on all the reasons why I should send Mama back to Mooreville, then hole up in the Peabody and let the police sort everything out. Right now all I want is a good hot bath.

We're just crossing the lobby when I spot the recently widowed H. Grayson Mims III leaving the hotel looking anything but bereaved. With him is a strange-looking woman I haven't seen among the dance competitors. He just jumped to the top of the suspect list.

"Lovie, quick. Follow him."

"Who?"

You can hear her all the way to New York. H. Grayson Mims glances back and I jerk Lovie behind the player piano.

"It's Babs' husband," I whisper. "With another woman."

I won't repeat what she says. Suffice it to say, if

Grayson heard, he'd fear for his prized body parts. Unfortunately an older woman who is passing by hears every word. She takes one disdainful look and indicts us on the spot.

"Riffraff," she sniffs. "Nowadays, there's no accounting who they let in this hotel."

Well, no wonder. My hair is uncombed, I'm wearing no makeup, and I'm still in sweats that got dragged through the fountain and other unmentionable debris. Lovie's not much better in her favorite lounge-about jeans that look like they came over on the Mayflower, and a baggy tee shirt with a slogan across the front that says KEEP AMERICA BEAUTIFUL, STAY IN BED.

Still, the snooty woman's no icon of fashion herself. I could tell her that painted-on eyebrows and hair teased to look like a football helmet went out of style in the seventies, but I won't stoop to her level.

Lovie has no such compunctions.

"Listen, you heifer. For your information, we're famous musicians." She plops on the piano stool and hits a few blues licks.

She could fool anybody. She's so good, she could even play on Beale Street. Aunt Minrose (may she rest in peace) was a concert pianist, and Lovie got every bit of her mother's talent.

"Come on." I tap her shoulder. "The suspect is getting away."

"I told you Babs' husband was the killer."

Lovie enjoys the last word. As we hurry after Grayson, Elvis trots along. He thinks it's a game and he's hamming it up, flashing his lopsided doggie smile and spreading his stage personality all over Memphis. There's no way to remain unnoticed.

A tired looking young mother tries to stop us so her two rambunctious children can pet him. It breaks my heart to tell her *Sorry, not today*, without even slowing down. I imagine Saint Peter is putting black marks by my name.

"He's headed to Beale Street, Lovie."

"What's he doing there this time of day?"

"Maybe a rendezvous with a hit man?"

Why else would a man be heading into a historic blues district at a time of morning when the stores aren't even open, the clubs are closed, and the jazzy music that floats from every open doorway is missing?

"But why take another woman?" Lovie has a point.

"Maybe she's in on it."

She looks the type, short and slinky with a bad dye job. If I weren't trying to nab her for murder, I'd tell her you don't put platinum streaks in black hair unless you want to look like a polecat. (Translation: *skunk*.)

The closer we get to Beale Street, the harder my heart pumps. And it has nothing to do with murder.

Jack and I honeymooned in Memphis. Every moment we didn't spend in our motel room (we couldn't afford the Peabody and stayed at a cheap stucco inn farther from the river), we explored Beale Street. Mr. Handy's Blues Hall and Silky O'Sullivan's, Black Diamond and Club 152, Tater Red's and A. Schwab's Dry Goods Store.

The Gibson Guitar Factory a few blocks away inspired Jack to buy a guitar, though he never did learn to play it with the same heart and soul he pours into the blues harp he always keeps in his pocket.

Don't get me started on Jack's harmonica or I'll end up bawling like a newborn calf.

I force myself to concentrate on Schwab's, which looks very much the way it did when it was built in 1876. You can find anything in there, from swizzle sticks to sweat pants. You can even get voodoo paraphernalia.

Jack bought me some *mojo hands,* lucky roots in oil that smell like dark secrets and night-scented moon flowers. I still have it.

Why is another question. When I get home, I really ought to clean out my house, get rid of the *mojo hands* and the dried roses from our wedding bouquet, the onyx angel he brought to me from heaven only knows where, the tin candy box with a carousel on top.

Moving on requires leaving behind baggage. At least that's what all the self-help books say. I'm not fully convinced those so-called experts are right. How can you know who you are if you don't remember where you've been? How can you ever learn anything about yourself if you just dump your past in the garbage can and forget about it?

"Quick, Callie." Lovie jerks me out of my reverie and into a doorway.

On top of everything else, I'm going to have a crick in my neck.

"The mark's stopped."

The minute we start sleuthing, she starts sounding like Sam Jaffe in *The Asphalt Jungle.* I half expect her to break out with a statement about crime being a cockamamie *form of human endeavor* or some such throwback to old crime movies. (In addition to Westerns, Lovie and I are partial to late night film noir.)

She risks a peek around the doorway. Taller by a good three inches, I peer over her head. Grayson has his arm around his female partner in crime and is talking earnestly to a street vendor.

"What's he saying?" Lovie asks.

"We'll bury him in the turnip patch. Do you know of any laws against that?"

"Thank you, Gloria Swanson." She's on to me. I've just paraphrased one of our favorites, *Sunset Boulevard*.

"How should I know what he's saying, Lovie? I don't have X-ray ears."

Up and down Beale, shop doors are beginning to open, the sun is climbing and I don't have my sunglasses. I'm beginning to regret my hasty decision to trail H. Grayson Mims. Shoot, I'm even regretting my decision to get out of bed. I should have told Elvis to just hold it.

The woman with H. Grayson opens her purse, takes out a pair of rhinestone-studded dark glasses, then swivels around and stares straight at us.

"Did she see us?" Lovie asks.

"If she did, what's she going to do? Turn us in for hunkering in a doorway? She doesn't even know who we are."

"I wouldn't count on it. I'm unforgettable."

Good grief. Here we go again.

"Forget it, Lovie. I don't think she even saw us."

Suddenly the "William Tell Overture" splits the

Peggy Webb

silence. We might as well have announced our presence with trumpet fanfare.

Grayson and cohort whirl around, and his hand shoots to his pocket. Holy cow. We're fixing to get shot in public (and probably in the heart, too) and my hair's not even combed.

Chapter 7

Beale Street Blues, Tattoos, and Wet Willie

In the split second it takes H. Grayson Mims to pull out his gun, my life flashes before my eyes. Might I add that I'm proud of what I see. Except for a few details. Which I don't have time to go into right now.

"Lovie! Duck!"

"It's just his billfold, Callie. He's buying bagels."

Listen, I don't care what he's doing. I'm changing my tune. Jerking my phone out of my pocket, I say *hello*. And I'm sorry to report I'm not very nice about it.

"You'll never guess what I heard." It's Mama sounding fully recovered from her brush with death. I wish I could say the same for myself.

"I can't talk now. I'm in the middle of something important"

"What could be more important than your mother?"

"Okay. What is it?" Major goal number one: learn to stand firm in the face of emotional blackmail.

"Fayrene and I were in that cute little gift shop in the lobby. You know, Lansky's? We heard Gloria Divine's the deposed princess of some foreign country."

"That's far-fetched, Mama. What foreign country?"

"What does it matter? She was probably assassinated."

Two murders on the same day in the same hotel do not add up to assassination, but I don't want to get into that with Mama. For one thing I'm tired and dirty. For another, all bedlam is breaking loose. Elvis is barking, Lovie is saying words she learned from bathroom walls, and Armageddon has started behind the door where we're skulking.

"I've got to go, Mama." I hang up on her, something I'm positive I'll live to regret. Behind us, the thundering, galloping noise is coming closer. "Down, Lovie!"

She drops and we hunker on the pavement like sewer mice faced with the world's biggest mousetrap. We don't have a single weapon, not even Lovie's baseball bat.

Rule number whatever-it-is: don't go sleuthing without a weapon. You never know when you'll land smack dab in the path of something meaner, uglier, and bigger than you.

The door behind us bursts open and I nearly wet my pants. Towering over us, seven feet if he's an inch, is the most fearsome man I've ever seen. Skin as slick and shiny as patent leather, dressed in black from head to toe, he looks like the funnel of a tornado. Even Lovie is intimidated.

"Well, well," he says. "What've we got here?"

I couldn't squeak if I were in the path of stampeding elephants. For once, even Lovie is rendered speechless.

"Don't ya'll move." Staring up at Giant Man's open mouth is like gazing into the abyss of a red stone canyon. "I'll be right back, sugar."

He turns around and thunders inside.

"*Sugar?*" Lovie gives me this look but I notice she's not moving.

"That's what he said."

I'm trying to decide whether to stay put, call the cops, or make a run for it. Suddenly the giant is back and all escape routes are closed.

"Here, ya'll." He's holding two enormous sandwiches in hands as big as Virginia hams. He even leans down and offers a biscuit to my dog. "Nobody goes hungry at Wet Willie's."

I'd give the food back, but I don't want to get on the bad side of a man twice the size of Arkansas. Besides, I don't want to hurt his feelings.

I accept the sandwich and say, "Thank you, sir."

My mama brought me up right.

Down the street at the Rum Boogie Café, a mournful trumpet signals the beginning of another day of nostalgia and blues. Soon throngs of people will pour onto Beale Street. I'm not about to stick around and be mistaken for a panhandler again.

"You're welcome, sugar. Ya'll have a nice day, now, you hear?"

I wonder if he's Wet Willie. It wouldn't be polite to ask. Lovie looks like she's going to anyway, and I give her a sharp nudge.

By the time our monumental benefactor leaves,

Grayson and his lady love are long gone. At this point, I don't even care. I've already hauled a dead body out of the fountain, been held at gunpoint by the police, and been mistaken for a beggar. And the day's not even half over.

I have an insane urge to go inside Wet Willie's and order the drink advertised on his windows— CALL A CAB. After a drink with a name like that, who would care if Grayson is cheating on his dead wife? Who would care if my sweats are so stiff with duck goo they could walk back to the Peabody by themselves? Who would care if Beale Street makes me think of a blues harp curled against the lips of a man who knows how to rock my world with a kiss?

"Let's go back to the hotel, Lovie." She's too busy eating to reply. "How can you eat? It's not even ten-thirty."

"If you'd forget the clock and eat when you're hungry, you might get some love handles, Callie."

I'm always after her to lose weight and she's always after me to gain. In a good-natured way, of course. Best friends since birth, we've never had a real fight.

Right now, though, I don't even want to get into a light-hearted discussion with Lovie over my love handles and all the name implies.

"Let's go, Lovie."

"Since we're here, we might as well go down the street to the tattoo parlor. We could get something cute and sassy to put on our hips. Maybe a little red devil with a halo. What do you think?"

"I think you're losing it. Come on."

"What's your hurry? Let's have some fun. Let's stop at the Rum Boogie Café and have a Long Island Ice Tea." Made with vodka, gin, rum, tequila, and Lord knows what else.

After the night and morning I've had, if I have a drink with that much alcohol in it, you might as well put me in a box and ship me back home to Eternal Rest. It's the best funeral home in Mississippi, even if my uncle does own it, and I sound like I'm bragging. But I'm not even sure Uncle Charlie's embalming skills could put some color back in my cheeks.

"Listen, Lovie. You stay here and have a Long Island Ice Tea if you want to, but I'm going back to the hotel and break into Grayson's room." He's somewhere on Beale Street with his new squeeze, and we'll never get a better chance.

"Now you're singing my song. Crime is the only thing that can make me leave off liquor." Lovie whips out her cell phone and punches in numbers.

"Who are you calling?"

"If we're going to cross crime tape, we need disguises and we need a diversion." Her connection goes through. "Bobby? I need a favor."

I start shaking my head and saying, "No, I don't want to involve Bobby." Naturally, she ignores me. When has Lovie ever listened to the voice of reason? Not that I'm always right. And there have been a few times (well, a lot, really) when I haven't used my own better judgment. Still, compared to Lovie, I'm a fount of discretion and wisdom.

"I need you and Fayrene to get in that crowd waiting for this morning's duck parade and create a ruckus. A big one."

Now that Lovie's pulled Fayrene into the investigation, Mama won't be far behind. I might as well find the Peabody's oven and stick my head in.

"Yep, that sounds good, Bobby. And I don't want you asking questions. 'Bye, now."

Good grief. Only she and Mama can get by with such high-handed behavior.

"What sounds good?"

"You don't want to know."

Holy cow. I'll bet it's criminal.

"Why do we need a diversion, Lovie?"

"So we can steal maid's uniforms."

"That ranks right up there with your hair-brained scheme to get Texas Elvis up in the hot air balloon, and we all know how that turned out." *Elvis impersonator fiasco*, and that's all I'm saying about that.

"Okay, Callie. You tell me how we're going to find a costume shop and get back here in time to ransack Grayson's room before he returns from his morning outing. We might as well send him a letter of intent."

She has a point, even if I don't like it. "Forget ransacking, Lovie. We're just going to *look*."

"You look, I'll pillage and plunder."

She's kidding. I hope.

Now that she's up to no good, Lovie trots along like somebody's set Memphis on fire and she has the only bucket of water. I try to keep up with her, but Elvis is determined to mark every light pole between Beale Street and the hotel.

Finally the Peabody comes into view, and Lovie whips out her phone again. "We're on the approach, Bobby. Get ready to rumble."

That sounds like something I don't want to be involved in. "What does that mean, Lovie?"

"Trust me. In a few minutes, this is all going down. Wait for my signal."

"I'm not going to stand here and argue with a criminal type," I paraphrase Richard Erdman to Dick Powell in *Cry Danger*.

Lovie shoots me a jump in the lake sign—to put a nice spin on it.

Elvis' Opinion #4 on Paw Prints, High Heel Sneakers, and Detectives at Large

This is my kind of morning. It reminds me of the old days of jumping on my motorcycle in the wee hours when fans were least likely to be waiting at Graceland's Music Gate, then roaring off for a few moments of stolen freedom.

Of course, adoring fans always caught up with me, just as they did this morning. There's no telling how many paw prints I'd have signed if we hadn't been in hot pursuit of H. Grayson Mims III.

By the time we get back to the hotel, the Peabody lobby is filling up with folks waiting for the duck parade. If I weren't deep undercover I'd prance over there and get the crowd rockin' 'n rollin' with "High Heel Sneakers." Listen, if Callie and Lovie would use me for the diversion, the crowd would be eating out of my paws. They could steal the angels off the top of the Peabody fountain and nobody would notice.

But I'm indispensable undercover. While they steal housekeeping uniforms, I'll be guarding the door. If anybody tries to bother Callie and Lovie in the middle of petty theft, he's liable to leave without a chunk of his leg.

Well, bless'a my soul.

Here comes Bobby at a fast lope with Fayrene puffing along behind. In that dark green getup, she looks like a mess of collard greens. Which just happens to be one of my favorite snacks, if you add a little ham hock.

Half hunkered behind an overstuffed sofa, we watch while Bobby and Fayrene get into place at a midpoint of the red carpet. (Red carpet for ducks, my substantial but cute backside!) Within seconds the crowd is in a milling, screeching turmoil.

If you ask me, that's not a diversion, that's a riot.

"Go," Lovie says, and we race toward the service area. Only one woman tries to stop us—the same nosey old broad we encountered earlier by the player piano.

Lovie snarls, "Out of my way, heifer," while Callie tries to smooth things over with, "Police business."

My human mom gets by with it. Barely.

If we're going to take up detective work as a sideline to beauty (Callie) and entertainment (Lovie and me), I'm going to suggest she order three faux badges imprinted with ECDL. Elvis and Company, Detectives at Large.

We skulk through a labyrinth of back rooms not suitable for the fainthearted till we find one with HOUSEKEEPING written over the door. I'm getting all psyched up to make my big contribution when Callie says, "Lovie, grab a couple of uniforms. I'll stand guard."

What does she think I am? A silly shih tzu? Believe me, she'll pay for this. I'm already working on a 3 A.M. urge to piss on a Union Avenue fire hydrant.

But since I am by nature a big-hearted dog, I relent enough to let Callie think she's doing all the guard duty.

"Hurry, Lovie," my human mom says, "I hear somebody coming."

I could have told her that two minutes ago. I'd know the smell of ducks anywhere. If that's not the duck master, it's somebody wearing eau de duck.

"I can't find my size," Lovie says.

"Just grab one. We've got to scram."

We do, and they head the wrong way. Naturally. With the sound of footsteps getting closer, they jump behind an icemaker, dragging yours truly. While they pray not to get caught (I can tell by their auras), I check out the situation.

Just as I thought. It's that dour man in his silly gold-braided suit heading down the hall toward the break room. Listen, I don't have to go down there to look. I can smell chocolate chip cookies and pepperoni pizza a mile away.

He's probably having to tank up on sugar and carbs before he goes up to the roof to bring those dratted ducks down. If I were in his tacky shoes, I'd have a little nip of something strong before I opened the door to the duck palace.

I get ready to attack in case he spots us, but he's in a hurry. I guess herding a bunch of moronic ducks around not only builds a big appetite, it gives you tunnel vision.

We wait till we hear the door down the hall slam

shut, then we charge up the stairs. Let me tell you, charging for four floors is no picnic.

"I've got dibs on the bathroom." Lovie dives in without waiting to see if anybody has a bigger need.

"Make it snappy," Callie says. "I'll be back in a minute."

What does she mean? Back in a minute?

I'm not long in finding out. Before I can say *pass the Pup-Peroni*, she's hustled me up to the tenth floor and asked Ruby Nell to *watch Elvis for a while*.

Watch Elvis, my crooked hind leg. Who does she think did all the work this morning? But do I get any thanks for it, any gold medals, any fried peanut butter and banana sandwiches?

All I get is a lousy pat on the head and the admonition to *be a good boy*.

If she thinks I'm going to behave while she runs off and has all the fun, she's got another think coming. I'm fixing to break out of this joint and head to Graceland where folks appreciate a dog of my iconic status.

Chapter 8

Maids, Mayhem, and Faux Fox Furs

When I get to her room, Mama's on the phone with Uncle Charlie, saying, "Everything's great and everybody's having a big time."

Apparently he buys it because she laughs at something he says, then tells him goodbye.

"Doesn't Uncle Charlie know about the murders?"

Gloria Divine's demise won't make the news till tonight, but I'm surprised he hasn't already heard about Babs Mabry Mims being pushed off the roof.

"Sometimes he falls asleep during the news. Charlie's getting old."

"Don't say that, Mama."

"Well, he is."

"You're practically the same age."

"Yes, but I put Preparation H on my wrinkles."

"Holy cow, Mama. That's for hemorrhoids."

"If it can shrink them, it can shrink anything."

On that shocking beauty note, I inquire if she'll

keep Elvis for a little while. Naturally Mama is full of questions I don't want to answer.

"Where are you going?"

"I can't tell you, Mama. Can you keep him or do you and Mr. Whitenton have other plans?"

"For your information, he's resting, and so am I."

I hope they're not planning to rest together, but judging by her sexy silk lounging outfit, I'm not too sure.

"Don't give me that look, Callie. Of course I can keep him. But I don't see why you can't tell me what you're planning to do."

"Just trust me. Okay?"

"What's such a secret you can't tell your own mother, who gave birth the hard way?"

I'd ask her what that means, but I don't have time. It could mean I'm facing a tough time if I ever get pregnant, but knowing Mama, it probably means she's just being dramatic.

"Gotta go, Mama." I kiss her cheek. "Bye Elvis. Be a good boy."

Elvis looks none too pleased at being left behind, but I can't help that. If I'd known this girls' getaway would turn into murder, I'd have left him home.

When I get back to our room, the TV is running full blast and Lovie is in the shower with the water faucets going wide open. I go into the bathroom and knock on the shower door. She jumps and says a word that causes a sonic boom.

"Hurry up, Lovie. We've got to go."

"Okay, okay. I'm coming."

Much as I'd love a good long soak in a hot tub, I

barely have time for a swipe with a damp wash-cloth. The only good thing I can say about my spit bath is that at least I'm not planning to get close to anybody. Translated, that's Champ and Jack, especially Jack.

As a matter of fact, I've made up my mind: I'm not having sex with him again even if he sends a year's supply of chocolates and six dozen of my favorite Gertrude Jekyll roses. The only thing that would make me relent is a certificate of sainthood and an ironclad commitment to fatherhood.

I go back into the bedroom and put on the tailored charcoal gray housekeeping uniform Lovie left on the bed, plus a cute pair of Juicy Couture ballerina flats. Investigative rule number one: always be prepared to run.

So far, that's my only rule, but if life keeps coating me with tar and tossing me in the briar patch, I'm liable to come up with a whole bunch of them.

On the TV, a perky newswoman who took somebody's bad advice about blue eye shadow prattles on about a ribbon cutting at the new Starbucks in Germantown.

Who cares about coffee when I'm wondering if I can fasten the buttons on my stolen disguise.

Miss Blue Eye Shadow says, "In apparently unrelated crimes, two women have been found dead at the Peabody." I listen for new information, but the TV news reporter doesn't say a thing I don't already know.

If I want to learn anything, it looks like I'll have to sneak around in an outfit that was made for somebody six inches shorter. Add a little white apron and I look like the star of a triple-X rated

French film. The only good thing I can say about this high-water costume is that the buttons fasten.

Lovie emerges from the bathroom as the most mind-boggling maid in the South.

"I look like a snow-capped mountain." She twirls around to inspect herself in the mirror. "Of course, more than one lucky man has skied down these slopes."

Lovie's eye-popping creamy magnolia flesh reminds me of all my clients who will benefit when I turn Hair.Net into a south-of-Mooreville Riviera. Listen, just because the place where you live is small doesn't mean you have to think small.

"I don't care what it costs, Lovie. As soon as we get home, I'm getting a tanning bed for Hair.Net."

I'll paint a mural on the wall with a blue wash of ocean and an inviting sweep of sandy beach. Maybe I can get some of those cute faux seagulls to add a touch of authenticity.

"Great, then I can look like a beach in Tahiti."

She's incorrigible.

I twist my hair into a tight bun, then perch a pair of reading glasses on my nose. Even my dog wouldn't know me. "Let's go, Lovie."

We race to the elevator, but when we get to the tenth floor we slow down. It won't do to act like women who have come to pick locks.

"Which way?" Lovie asks.

"1016. I hope." There is no crime tape. Apparently the cops have already removed it. Not surprising since this is only a secondary crime scene.

She says words that shake tall buildings. "If we break into the wrong room looking like this, we're liable to be captured and sold into white slavery."

"Dream on," I tell her. "More like a sideshow at the circus."

She heads off in the opposite direction. That's not like her, to huff off mad.

"Lovie, wait. Where are you going?"

"Be right back."

She moves really fast for a woman her size. Before I can work up a nervous sweat, she has raced down the hall and nabbed the cart around the corner.

"Props," she says. "Besides, we need the rubber gloves."

She starts picking the lock while I act as lookout.

"Lovie, wait." I give a sharp knock and assume my best French accent (which has Mooreville written all over it). "Housekeeping!"

Lovie says a word not meant for polite company. "Who do you think is going to be in there? The occupant's dead and they probably moved her husband to another room."

"He could be back."

That takes the starch out of her sails. When there's no answer, she recovers, then resumes breaking and entering.

"Hurry, Lovie. Somebody's coming."

Her hairpin slips and she has to start all over.

"Quick, Cal. Do something."

What am I supposed to do? Stick a thumb out and pretend to be hitchhiking?

The footsteps get closer, and a gentleman in a dark blue suit rounds the corner. I grab the cart, twist it around to hide Lovie's nefarious activities, then lean over and pretend to be looking for soap.

Anxiety always makes me sweat. I feel damp patches forming on my borrowed finery.

I also feel a hard pinch on my behind. If Jack were here, he'd knock this man into next Sunday. Even easygoing Champ wouldn't put up with that kind of misbehavior. Of course, I don't need them. I take pride in my independence.

"Back off, mister."

I whirl the cart around to block the interesting view caused by my short skirt. And while I'm at it, I make sure to run over his toe.

Mr. No Gentleman lets out a word that is not so nice.

"Oh, I'm sooo sorry." I can do molasses-through-magnolias Southern as well as the next belle. "Do you need me to call anger management?"

He storms off without a word. While I'm wondering if he's going to report me, Lovie jerks me into the room, cart and all, and slams the door.

"I thought you were going to get us both landed in the pokey," she says.

"You told me to do something."

"I didn't mean act like the fastest gun in the West." Lovie starts going through drawers. "Why couldn't you just say 'eat your heart out' and then stand there looking wonderful?"

I could get huffy and argue, but she's just said I look wonderful. Besides, I'm like a heat-seeking missile. I never let myself get sidetracked. (Well, hardly ever, unless I'm feeling vulnerable and Jack shows up and starts spreading sweet talk like strawberry jam.)

"Make sure you don't get anything out of its place."

I stroll across the room to the closet and pull open the door. Jackpot.

"Lovie, you'd better come over here."

The closet is stuffed with furs, some of them faux, some real. Everything is here, from a full-length mink to a silver fox stole to a faux leopard walking coat. I instantly take umbrage. Listen, if I draped myself in animal skins, Elvis would disown me.

While I'm stewing, Lovie's looking at tags.

"There's more than eighty thousand dollars' worth of fur in this closet," she says, "and every bit of it is from Goldsmith's."

"Which means Babs Mims bought them all right here, probably after they arrived. If these are hers."

"Which means it would take a very rich man to keep up with her spending habits."

"Keep searching, Lovie. See if you can find a receipt. Anything that will let us know we're in the right room."

I head toward the bathroom. Toiletries are piled in an untidy heap on the counter and the usual wet towels are on the floor. The real housekeeping staff could be here any minute to make up this room.

I kick towels out of my way and paw through the mess. If this is Babs' room, Grayson hasn't bothered to pack up her stuff. Maybe he's too grief stricken. Or is he too guilty?

The toiletries tell no stories. I reach for a small pink quilted cosmetic case. Inside is a bottle of sleeping pills. The label says Babs Mabry Mims.

I put the pills back where I found them and call through the door, "She was a pill popper." There's no answer. "Lovie? Did you hear me?"

Still no answer. A chill spreads through me. Picturing Lovie bound and gagged, I grab the nearest weapon—a ten-ounce can of hairspray. Whoever is out there had better watch out. I'm a whiz with beauty products. If I can't blind him (temporarily, of course) with hydrofluorocarbons, I can raise a sizable knot on his head with the can.

Easing around the door frame, I spot Lovie sitting on the bed, mesmerized by something in her hand. From across the room it looks like a bill of some kind.

"Lovie?"

She jumps, then whirls around and sees me.

"Shoot, Callie. You scared me to death."

"What have you got?"

"You don't want to know."

She hands it to me anyway, a small photograph featuring two smiling young women—Babs and someone I don't know—with their arms around a man I know only too well.

"Mr. Whitenton!"

"I warned you."

"Good grief, Lovie. If he killed Babs, he could be after Mama."

"Exactly. Let's go ransack his room."

"We can't. He's there."

"Doing what? Planning his next murder?"

"Resting, Mama said."

I stare at the picture to see if I've missed something. Mr. Whitenton's hair is darker and he looks younger, maybe by four or five years. There's nothing to identify the place except the rose print wallpaper and food-laden antique sideboard behind them. This is an intimate setting, somebody's house, maybe after a holiday meal.

"I say we roust him out of bed and wring a confession out of him."

Lovie's only half kidding. She adores her Valentine kin, particularly Mama, and wouldn't hesitate to beat somebody up for her.

"This photograph doesn't prove anything," I tell her. "Except that Thomas Whitenton knew the first murder victim."

"Why didn't he mention it?" Lovie has a point.

"Maybe he's covering up something, but we have an eyewitness who saw Grayson push Babs."

"You think he killed his wife over a fur splurge?"

"People have been killed for less, Lovie. Besides, we have no connection between Thomas and Gloria."

"Then what are we waiting for, Sherlock?" Lovie stands up and tugs her skirt down. Unsuccessfully, I might add. There's too much Lovie and too little skirt. "Let's hit Gloria's room."

"Wait a minute. Where did you get this picture?"

"Babs's purse."

It's on the bed beside her, wide open. Lovie picks it up and snaps it shut.

At the same time, there's an ominous click at the door. With my heart in my throat, I turn around just in time to see the handle turning. Holy cow! We're in deep trouble now. Lovie's holding a dead woman's purse and I'm standing here with her picture.

"Quick, Lovie. Do something."

Chapter 9

Carts, Clues, and Cahoots

I don't know what I expected Lovie to do, but certainly not this. While I'm watching the door handle turn and calculating how much longer I have to live as a free woman, Lovie hauls off and leaps into the cart. Babs' purse and all.

"Let's get out of here," she says, then pulls the sheets and towels on top of her.

Shoot! Till now Lovie has always taken center stage. Why didn't I think to jump in the cart and leave her to face the music? She's much better at lying her way out of a situation than I am.

"Callie?" From all those layers of linens, she sounds like a hissing snake. If she were, I'd be Cleopatra. Rather than die at the hands of enemies, I'd reach in, grab a lethal viper, and hold it to my breast.

Frozen with terror and indecision, I watch the door slowly move inward.

A hand reaches out of the linens and snatches

the picture. I look down to see Lovie glaring up at me.

"Move it!"

I do—just as H. Grayson Mims strolls through the door. With none other than Victor Mabry's wife plastered on his arm.

Just how many women is this man consorting with? First polecat, and now this.

When he sees me, he drops her arm and moves a discreet distance away. Thank goodness, he's too rattled—probably at being seen with another woman so soon after his wife's death—to notice that underneath the too-short maid's uniform, the hasty French twist and the reading glasses is the woman he asked to dance the first night of the competition.

"I didn't expect housekeeping to get here so soon after the crime tape came down. Did you leave plenty of towels?"

"Yes sir." If he wants to look on the floor and doesn't mind that they're dirty. By the time he discovers all that, I'll be long gone.

Calling on acting skills from second grade (I played a petunia), I careen past Grayson, run over his shoes, bump into the doorway, backtrack and call on every deity I know (but only silently). Finally I gain the hallway.

The minute the door closes behind me, I lift the top towel and snarl at Lovie. "Get out of there."

She climbs out, looking disheveled and not the least bit sorry.

"Do you know how much this cart weighs with you in it?"

"As much as a beached whale?"

"That's not funny, Lovie. Next time I'll jump in and you push."

"It had to be me. I'm memorable."

I hope she means because of her wild red hair, but I wouldn't bet on it.

"Ask any of my former lovers," she says, erasing all doubt. She grabs a glass and presses it to the door. "Let's see what lover boy's up to."

More cautious by nature than my bold cousin, I check the hallway first to make sure we're in the clear. Then I grab another glass from the cart and use it as a makeshift earphone.

Whatever Grayson and Babs' first husband's wife are doing, they're doing it quietly. I can't hear a thing except an occasional low hum of voices followed by long silences that make me sweat. What if they're not having a conversation about murdering Babs? What if they're having a conversation about snuffing out two nosey women posing as maids?

"Let's get out of here, Lovie," I whisper.

"Wait. I think I heard something about Babs' furs."

"That's hearsay. It won't stand up in a court of law."

"We're not testifying in a court of law. We're just trying to save Aunt Ruby Nell."

I'd concede the point if she hadn't jumped into the housekeeping cart and made me push.

"We won't live long enough to save anybody if Grayson discovers dirty towels on his floor."

"I didn't think of that." She grabs the cart and starts down the hall.

"Leave it here, Lovie."

"Can't. Babs' purse is inside."

Not to mention her picture. Shoot. If I'm going to keep running into dead bodies everywhere, I'm going to have to quit taking things from the murder scene.

"Where to?" Lovie asks.

My back is stiff from hunkering down in front of Grayson's door; my throat is dry from arguing with Lovie in a whisper, and I don't even want to think about the trouble we'll be in if we get caught parading around the Peabody in stolen uniforms, breaking into the other guests' rooms.

But I'm a Valentine through and through. Nothing can stop me now. Unless it's an act of God.

"Charge forth, Lovie. Gloria's room. If we can find a connection between her and Mr. Whitenton, I think we've found the killer."

"Which way?"

"Next door. 1014."

"How do you know?"

"I overheard the woman who registered the dancers talking about it."

We move a few feet down the hall. With the cart covering her criminal doings and me standing guard, Lovie whisks out the tool of her trade, a bent hairpin, and sets to work. Who should come down the hall by an act of God but Fayrene, in full green splendor.

"Callie? Is that you?"

She's yelling like I'm at the other end of a football stadium. Is there anybody east of the Mississippi River who didn't hear her? Any minute I expect doors to pop open and vigilante guests to turn us in.

"Hey, Fayrene," I say. "I thought you and Bobby were at the duck parade."

"We already did our pre-parade diversion like Lovie said. I need my scarves for the big performance."

I don't think Lovie meant for them to disrupt the parade, but I don't want to stand in the hall discussing that with Fayrene.

"How's it going down there? Did you hear anything about the murders?"

"Enough to put me in a state of conservation."

I hope she means consternation, but with Fayrene you never can tell.

"Somebody at the duck parade said the Peabody murders were so bad they were going to call out the Highway Control. And they're fixing to test the victims for NBA. No telling who will be next."

Over the rim of the cart, Lovie shoots me a look and I mouth, "DNA." She explodes, then tries to cover her laughter with a cough.

Fayrene puts her hand over her heart. "Lord, Lovie, I didn't see you. You nearly gave me a frustration attack. Are you okay, hon?"

"Fine." Lovie sputters some more. "Frog in my throat."

"Gargle with saltwater. That's the best."

Fayrene purses her lips the way she does when she's standing behind the checkout counter at Gas, Grits, and Guts, getting ready to find out juicy tidbits she can pass along to her customers. I hold my breath and ask the gods of wacky women to intervene.

"Well, you two get back to whatever you were doing. I've got to get back to the duck carpet and put on the rest of my show."

Thank goodness she's gone. When I get home I'm going to thank the universe by lighting a white candle under a full moon.

Fayrene trots a few steps, then turns back to me. "Hon, I don't like to criticize, you being a beauty operator and all, but gray's not your color."

"Thanks for being honest, Fayrene."

Lovie and I stand there like two barber poles till she's out of sight, then Lovie cracks up.

"Hush. We're going to attract attention and somebody's going to call the Highway Control."

"She's right, you know." Lovie inserts her hairpin into the lock.

"About what?"

"Gray's not your color."

"I may have to kill you."

"Stand in line."

The lock springs open and we cross crime scene tape. Thank goodness, nobody sees us enter.

"Lovie, you check out the drawers while I check the closet."

For a competitive dancer, Gloria packed light. Mama and Fayrene shop for weeks before they attend one of these competitions, then spend days planning their dance costumes as well as their clothing for the other fancy occasions.

Did Gloria expect to go on a spending splurge here with a sugar daddy (maybe Thomas) to foot the bill? Or do all these drab dresses mean she was trying to blend into the wallpaper? If so, what did she have to hide?

Even her shoes are unexciting, low-heeled beige pumps. Not very colorful clothing for a woman who was killed in a Technicolor outfit.

This Gloria was a woman of mystery. It looks like she was a woman who sought to dazzle onstage but didn't want to be noticed in her everyday life.

"Find anything, Lovie?"

"Nothing but underwear and a bag of candy."

"What kind?"

"Hershey's kisses."

"I meant the underwear."

"Bikini thongs. Black lace. Why?"

"If we know more about the victim, it might help us find the killer."

Lovie holds the thongs in front of her uniform. "Looks like she's my kind of woman."

She tosses the lingerie back into the drawer, then peels the wrapper from a piece of chocolate and pops it into her mouth.

"Good grief. You're eating evidence."

"Evidence of what? The bag was open. And I took only one." She reaches in again. "Okay, three." She rolls the bag up and tosses it back into the drawer. "Nobody's going to miss them. Besides, I think the cops have bagged and tagged all the good stuff."

I think she's right. If the police have removed evidence, they've been thorough. Still, we check the bathroom in case they missed something.

Gloria has used only one towel and one wash-cloth, and they're hung neatly over the shower rod. The real surprise here is her stash of cosmet-ics. Showgirl stuff. Heavy pancake base, glitter eye shadow, long-lasting lipstick, and false fingernails and eyelashes.

"What do you make of it, Callie?"

I defer to Lovie about food and she defers to me about beauty. If I know anything, I know my beauty products. Ask anybody in Mooreville.

"She was either making the mistake of trying to hide her age under too much makeup, or she was in show business."

"If she was a showgirl, Thomas might have known her."

"That's possible. Now all we have to do is figure out why he killed them."

Chapter 10

Surprise Visitor, News from Home, and Family Quarrels

The "William Tell Overture" nearly sends me through the ceiling. Lovie says a word that could get us permanently barred from polite company. It's Uncle Charlie calling.

"Hello, dear heart. I'm in Memphis."

"I'm relieved, Uncle Charlie. You heard about the murders?"

"Yes, and Ruby Nell's narrow escape."

"Did Mama call you?"

"No, Jarvetis did. Fayrene told him everything. I'm here to take Ruby Nell home."

"Good. It's getting dangerous here. With all the threats to Mama, Lovie and I are trying to see what we can find out."

"You and Lovie be careful. I'll get a report later."

"Where are you now, Uncle Charlie?"

"Parking. Which room is Ruby Nell's?"

"It's 1034. We'll meet you there in case you need a support team. Mama can be stubborn."

"You're not telling me anything I don't know, dear heart."

"How are Hoyt and the cats?"

"In good hands. I left them in Champ's care. See you later, dear heart."

I'm glad to hear that a vet with Champ's credentials and love of animals is looking after my pets. And not just because I care about them. As long as Champ has responsibilities in Mooreville, he won't be driving to Memphis to clip my wings.

Not that he'd want to curb me in any personal way, but I don't think he'd be too happy with my amateur detective activities, especially if he knew the whole truth. He's the kind of man who likes to keep people and animals safe—a wonderful quality in a potential daddy. Unless "safe" means "under your thumb."

Mama and Uncle Charlie (Daddy, too, from what I remember) let me explore all over the farm without supervision. Never once did they tell me not to climb a tree for fear of falling or investigate a bird's nest for fear of snakes. The only thing they did say was, "Stay out of the lake."

If Jack had children, he'd be like the Valentines. He'd encourage adventure.

See, that's why I'm in such a dilemma about my future. I have this Champ-versus-Jack daddy-argument with myself all the time. Not that Jack has expressed any interest in being a daddy.

I swear, this internal tug of war is wearing me out.

"Why was Daddy calling?" Lovie asks. I could hug her for sidetracking me. When I tell her, she says, "Aunt Ruby Nell won't go."

"I don't know. Uncle Charlie can be stubborn, too. Let's change clothes and find out who wins. Besides, I have to get Elvis."

As I head toward the door, Lovie yells, "Wait." Reaching into the cart, she retrieves Babs' purse and the photograph.

"I had forgotten about those. Now what?"

"Take evidence now, deal with it later."

"I don't like it, but you're right. We can't risk going back to Babs's room. Grayson might not be so congenial this time. We'll just have to add another theft to our growing list of crimes."

Since our uniforms leave no room to hide evidence, Lovie drops the picture in the purse, slings it over her arm, and sashays down the hall acting natural, while I ditch the cart looking furtive. I never was much of a performer, even as a second grade petunia.

We're almost to the elevator when two women see us and yell, "Yoohoo." I punch the elevator button again, but it's stuck on the fifth floor. And they're coming at a fast trot.

"Busted," I say, and Lovie says, "Buck up."

They catch up with us, panting. It's *pink foam rollers* and *beige housecoat*, the two ladies I heard giving evidence after I fished Gloria from the fountain.

Foam Rollers taps my arm. "We need some more shampoo in room 1020."

Lovie punches me and I grunt. "We're off duty."

"What would one little shampoo hurt? I saw the cart."

I punch Lovie and she says, "It's against the rules."

"If you ask me, there are too many rules in this world and not enough common sense." Foam Rollers pulls her glasses down and peers over the top. "Say, don't I know you?"

"No ma'am. I don't do your room."

Fortunately, the elevator arrives. Unfortunately, the two women get on, then stand there expectantly like naughty puppies, waiting their chance to pounce.

I punch Lovie and nod toward the fire exit.

"Aren't you getting on?" Foam Rollers asks. For a minute I think she's going to grab my arm and drag me into the elevator.

"I forgot my toothbrush."

The doors shish shut on two puzzled eye-witnesses.

"For Pete's sake, Callie. Your toothbrush?"

"I don't function well under stress. Speaking of which . . . I'm going to have a heart attack if we don't get out of here."

I dash toward the stairwell and take the stairs two at a time with Lovie puffing along behind me. She's saying words I don't want to ever hear again.

"It's only six floors, Lovie, and it's all downhill."

"I don't care if it's two and the stairs are slicked with pig grease. If I wet my pants before we get to the room, it's all your fault."

Lovie's all bark and no bite. If she thought anybody was placing blame on me (whether it belonged or not), she'd be the first to pick up her baseball bat and threaten a walloping.

"Why didn't you go in Gloria's bathroom?"

"Hush up, Callie. I can't talk and hold it in at the same time."

We make it back to our room on the fourth floor without encountering anybody else, which is a very good thing. Judging by the "forgot my toothbrush" remark, I've used up my last good lie.

Lovie bursts toward the bathroom while I shed my maid getup and change into a pair of Audrey Hepburn skinny pants, a cute pair of Michael Kors ballerina flats, and my favorite yellow cotton turtleneck that brings out the highlights in my brown, shoulder-length bob.

Trust Lovie to get into a pair of outrageous cowboy boots and her usual low-cut getup that bares a mind-boggling amount of cleavage. She flops onto the bed, boots and all.

"We have to go, Lovie."

"Why?"

"Because . . ."

Elvis needs me? Mama needs me? I've spread myself all over everybody's needs today except my own. Kicking off my shoes, I plop onto the covers beside Lovie.

"You're right. Uncle Charlie's here. Let him take care of everybody for a while."

"I wish I had some potato chips."

"You've got enough in the closet to feed a small third world country."

"Yeah, but I'm too tired to get them." Lovie gives me a smile nobody can resist. "Pretty please?"

I unfold my long legs and go over to rake through her stash of junk food in the closet.

"Barbecue or plain?"

"Both."

I toss her two bags, then get one for myself. Ordinarily I snack on carrots and apples and strawberries and yogurt. Since I've started sleuthing, I've developed an appetite for food that is not good for me. Or maybe the craving developed about the time Jack left.

"Lovie, do you think I'm making a mistake with Jack?"

"You mean divorcing him or still sleeping with him?"

"Both, I guess."

"No, on both counts."

"Yeah, but shouldn't a woman planning to divorce a man not have these urges?"

"Cut yourself some slack, Callie. The day I don't have those urges, you can put me six feet under."

"I need you to be serious, Lovie. My personal life is so chaotic it's driving me crazy."

Lovie sits straight up, cross-legged, her boots making a wild red statement against the bedspread. She wraps her hands around mine, and I feel like a baby bird being enveloped in its mother's wing. This is the thing I love most about Lovie. When it really counts, she always comes to your rescue.

"You listen to me, Cal, and you listen good. Nobody is perfect. Nobody makes the right decisions all the time. But if you listen with your heart instead of your brain, nine times out of ten, everything will turn out okay."

"You think?"

"I know."

The way Lovie says it, I believe her. We lean against the pillows, finish our chips, and breathe. Simply breathe.

Without saying a word, we both know when it's

time to go. We get off the bed, dust off the crumbs, and head to the door.

"I feel like a better human being," Lovie says.

"I do, too."

"Potato chips will do it every time."

Trust Lovie to make light of her part in smoothing balm on a wounded cousin.

By the time we arrive at Mama's room on the tenth floor, the fireworks have already begun. The sound of angry words between Mama and Uncle Charlie halts us in our tracks.

We stand outside the door like little children caught with our hands in the cookie jar. And we don't even need a glass at the door to hear every word.

"I'm taking you home, Ruby Nell."

"Over my dead body, Charlie Valentine."

"In that case . . ." We hear a big clatter that sounds like bricks being chunked against the floor. ". . . I'm staying."

"The hotel's booked."

"I'll stay here."

"Not in this room, you don't."

"I promised my brother I'd take care of you, and nobody's going to stop me."

"You're a stubborn old jackass."

"You think you can get around me with sweet talk?"

Holy cow! What has happened to my family? First Jack leaves, then true love comes to Lovie and she's too stubborn to see it, and now this.

Until Mama took up with Mr. Whitenton, Uncle Charlie and Mama rarely argued. Even when they did, it was more like an exchange you'd see on a

TV sitcom, a mild-mannered disagreement you knew would turn out all right in the end. She'd pout and he'd say, "Now, now, dear heart," and she'd end up doing things her way anyhow and then inviting him to a reconciliation Sunday dinner of fried chicken.

I'd like things to be the way they were, but I guess change comes whether you want it or not. The trick to survival is to be resilient enough to bend with the winds and swim with the tides.

"It sounds like Armageddon in there, Lovie. What are we going to do?"

"You tell me. I've never heard Daddy like this. He never gets upset at me, even when I give him good cause."

"We'd better get in there."

My hand is already lifted to knock when Mama and Uncle Charlie start laughing.

I can't take much more of this roller coaster Memphis visit. If things get any more complicated, I may have to jump off the top of the Peabody.

Elvis' Opinion #5 on Gossip, Family, and Soul Dogs

Things were getting boring around here till Charlie showed up and chunked his bags into Ruby Nell's closet. She was painting her toenails and I was trying to think up a way I could finagle my way off the floor and into the middle of her comfy bed when he burst in. Bursting in is not Charlie Valentine's usual style. He's the laid-back type who strolls and quotes Shakespeare and builds bridges over everybody else's troubled waters. (Listen, I know my Simon and Garfunkel. Talented guys, but they couldn't hold a candle to me.)

Turns out, Charlie heard about the murders on TV and he was trying to decide whether to drive to Memphis. Then Jarvetis called to report Fayrene's version of her brush with death as well as the attack on Ruby Nell, and Charlie charged north like General Robert E. Lee.

There's nothing like the power of gossip to stir things up.

Ruby Nell acts like she's not happy to see him, but don't let her blustery act fool you. He's been her anchor ever since Michael Valentine went to that big Graceland in the Sky. (I was there myself before they sent me back in this suave dog suit.)

If Ruby Nell would ever sit still long enough for a little self-examination, she might be surprised at what she'd discover.

Big changes are afoot with this family, and I'm not talking about Luke Champion. Don't get me wrong. I like him. He's a good vet and he's going beyond the call of duty to keep Callie's silly strays, especially Hoyt. But if he wants me to put in a good word for him, he'd best be finding ways to keep that dumb cocker spaniel in Mantachie. Permanently.

If Callie had her way, every stray cat and dog in Mooreville would end up on little satin doggie-and-cat pillows beside her bed. She can't say no to anybody, including the women who sit in her beauty shop chair, spill their sob stories, and walk out the door with fresh haircuts and interest-free loans.

One of my missions in life is to keep the coast clear of freeloaders and animal riffraff so I can work in peace. Listen, I'm here for a lofty purpose—to teach my human mom to love herself. It's all well and good to be Mooreville's answer to Mother Teresa and Oprah, but Callie's got to learn to draw the line so she can make room for her own dreams.

I know it looks hopeless right now, but that's where yours truly comes in.

I sashay over and plop my philosophical self

right in front of Ruby Nell's door. When Callie comes in, she'll see me first. I'll do a few "Hound Dog" moves and she'll smile and scratch behind my ears.

And for a little while, my human mom will experience the sheer joy of a true heart connection. Listen, I know it's just a connection with her soul dog, but you have to start somewhere.

Chapter 11

Separate Beds, Bad News, and Latoya LaBelle

When Lovie and I walk in, Uncle Charlie's bags are in Mama's closet and he's turning down her other bed. I'm glad to see he's staying here. Believe me, as long as Charles Sebastian Valentine is in this room, Mr. Whitenton won't get within ten feet of Mama.

Still, Uncle Charlie has always been a sort of benevolent godfather, protecting Mama and me from a distance with the lines clearly drawn. Now the lines are blurring between him and Mama, and I don't know what to make of it.

The only thing normal about this scene is Elvis waiting for me with his usual sweet doggie grin and his tail thumping. Sometimes, if it weren't for the simple pleasures and uncomplicated connections with my basset and my other dear animals, I think I'd shatter into small pieces.

"Hello, dear hearts." When Uncle Charlie comes over to Lovie and me, it's like hugging a ticking bomb. If I didn't know better, I'd say my uncle was a dangerous man.

"What did you find out?" he asks, and Mama jumps out of her chair.

"What do you mean, *what did you find out?*" Mama's question is strictly rhetorical. She's too smart not to guess what we've been up to, and she's flashing fire. "Carolina Valentine Jones, the next time you sneak off to have fun without me, I'm marking you off my Sunday dinner list."

"I wasn't off having fun. I'm trying to protect you, Mama."

"Flitter! I was taking care of myself before you were born. If I want to be mollycoddled, I'll hire a cute young man in tights and a red cape."

"Way to go, Aunt Ruby Nell." Lovie picks up Mama's fingernail polish. "I like this color. Do you mind if I use it?"

"Help yourself."

As the only man in our small Valentine circle (and I don't even want to think about why), Uncle Charlie is used to dealing with a room full of estrogen. But he has not endured this latest exchange with his usual calm. There's a look about him of a man with too much on his mind and a deep reluctance to express it.

"Mama, I was going to tell you anyway."

"After the fact," she says.

"Ruby Nell." Uncle Charlie speaks quietly—without adding *dear heart.* A look passes between them and Mama shrugs, then takes a pack of cigarettes out of her purse and lights up. She never smokes unless she's mad and wants to make her point, mainly that she's her own boss.

I've learned to curb my fears of blackened lungs and massive strokes and putting my mother in an early grave in favor of not arguing with her about her small defiant gesture. This so-called dance competition has been such a trying time, I'm about ready to take up bad habits myself.

I pick up my dog and sit on the edge of the bed. Telling bad news is easier if you're holding onto somebody who loves you. I know, *I know*. Most folks would say "but he's just a dog." Listen, he's a living, breathing creature, a miracle of this universe just like the rest of us. Best of all, his heart is loyal, something you don't find every day.

"I found a picture of Thomas Whitenton," I tell them. "With Babs and another woman."

Mama blows a puff of smoke my way, but for once she doesn't defend him.

"Was the other woman anybody you know?" Uncle Charlie asks.

"No, but I just got a quick glimpse. She looked about Babs' age." I start trying to describe her, and Lovie pulls the picture out of her purse. Why didn't I think of bringing it? She never ceases to amaze me.

Mama snatches the photo from Lovie and puffs away while she studies it. We can hardly see her for the fog of smoke. I think she's doing it deliberately.

All of us watch her and not even Uncle Charlie dares ask if she knows the other woman.

Finally she says, "Flitter," which could mean anything, then walks to the window and turns her back to us. I know this ploy. She knows something we don't, but she's going to make us work for the information.

Uncle Charlie is the one who comes to the rescue.

"Do you know her, Ruby Nell?"

"If I had been in on all the fun, I could have told you in the first place."

"Holy cow, Mama. Just tell us who it is."

"Thomas' niece."

"You never mentioned a niece. Did she, Lovie?"

Lovie lifts her right foot and admires her freshly painted toenails from all angles. Probably giving herself time to come up with an answer that will placate me and not get her on Mama's bad side.

"Maybe. Maybe not. I don't recall. My memory's not what it used to be." Lovie picks up a *Vogue* magazine Mama brought and proceeds to fan her toenails.

I'm so mad I hope she puts her boots on before her polish dries. "Why didn't he mention a niece when we had Sunday dinner together?" I ask. "Are you sure she's his niece, Mama?"

"For Pete's sake, Carolina. You sound like the Gestapo. Thomas' friends and relatives are nobody's business."

"Murder is everybody's business, Ruby Nell." Uncle Charlie retrieves the photo and sticks it in his pocket.

Now what? Lovie and I were planning to sneak the picture as well as the purse back to Babs' room before Grayson Mims put out an alarm for stolen property.

"Oh, all right, Charlie. Have it your way." Mama stubs her cigarette out and I grab another of Mama's magazines to fan out the smoke. "Thomas' niece went to Memphis State with Babs. They were in the same sorority. When Babs and his niece get together, Thomas sometimes sees them."

"Not anymore," Lovie drawls. I guess she's trying to make up for not taking my side with Mama. It works, too. When she puts her boots back on, I cross my fingers that she won't smear her fresh polish.

"Thomas wouldn't hurt a fly." Mama fiddles around in her purse for another cigarette, then changes her mind, thank goodness. "I may be prejudiced but I'm no bad judge of character. If you want to find the killer, you'd better look somewhere besides the room next to mine."

She flounces around, snatching up her robe and shower cap. "Now, everybody get out of here so I can take a bath."

"Do what you want, Ruby Nell. I'm staying. You can shut the bathroom door." Uncle Charlie plants himself in the room's only wing chair like an oak tree putting down roots.

The mood Mama's in, I'm relieved to let him deal with her. Besides, Lovie and I have plans. If we're going on another fact-finding foray, we'll need wigs. I want Lovie's memorable hair covered because I have no intention of pushing her around again in a housekeeping cart.

I'm just about to consult Uncle Charlie about our plans when there's a huge ruckus at the door—pounding and screeching and stomping. Uncle Charlie bolts across the room to check it out.

"Fayrene and Bobby," he tells us. Then he opens the door and they tumble into the room.

"Lord, Ruby Nell." Fayrene flies into the room trailing enough green scarves to do a dance of the seven veils. She presses her hand over her heart and flops onto Mama's bed. "My blood pressure's so high you might have to call an avalanche."

Now what? If Mooreville's answer to Mrs. Malaprop is calling for an ambulance, this can't be good. She swoons while Bobby jumps around her like a cricket on a hot sidewalk.

I'd be running for a wet washcloth, but I can tell she's faking it. Like Mama, Fayrene is partial to the dramatic gesture.

"What happened?" Uncle Charlie says.

"Somebody tried to strangle me, that's what. Tell them, Bobby. I'm too upset to talk."

"We were standing there watching the duck parade and Fayrene was making a big commotion, like Lovie told us to."

I'm hanging on to my splintered nerves, hoping he'll get to the point, when Fayrene recovers enough to sit up and steal his show.

"I was ransacking my purse. Complaining real loud. Acting like I couldn't find my cell phone and was fixing to haul off and pitch a hissy fit. All of a sudden . . ."

She jumps off the bed and begins prancing around the room, waving her arms and grimacing. There are rumors floating around Mooreville that she would have gone into show business if she hadn't married a man who loved birddogs more than Broadway. I wonder if the stories are true.

". . . somebody comes at me from behind. I feel

my own scarves tightening around my neck, choking the life out of me. Lord, I thought Jarvetis was going to have to plan my urology."

"Are you saying you think somebody tried to kill you?" Fayrene's ramblings always bother Uncle Charlie. He likes order and precision, clear-cut speech and logical behavior.

"I don't think. I *know*. If it hadn't been for my strong consternation, I'd be dead."

I don't know about Fayrene's constitution, but mine has about had it. I'm just getting ready to signal Lovie when Bobby drops the real bomb.

"A woman named Latoya LaBelle's dead. Strangled during the duck parade with her own scarf."

Chapter 12

Mocha, Madness, and Missives from Afar

The news divides Mama's room into two camps: the hysterics (Mama, Fayrene, and Bobby) and the rest of us. While the hysterics talk about the funeral they almost had to plan and the grief they almost had to bear, the rest of us discuss the latest murder and its ramifications.

For one thing, Uncle Charlie wants to know who the third victim is and whether she has a connection to the other two. Fortunately I recall the conversation I overheard in the lobby in the wee hours this morning about Gloria's friend with the strange name.

"Could *Lalique* and Latoya LaBelle be the same person?" I ask.

"If so, then the two latest victims were connected," Lovie says.

Uncle Charlie agrees. "The larger question, though, is who knew all three and who had motive to kill them?" He glances toward the threesome on the bed, now in a huddle about the most flattering color for Fayrene to wear in the casket. She's holding out for her usual green, Mama is arguing it will make her face look pallid, and Bobby is insisting that Ruby Nell is the one in danger.

"Good grief." I'm almost ready to join the hysterics myself. There are too many people in this room and I haven't had enough sleep, a good bath, a substantial meal. Besides, I do makeup for the dead. Mama knows good and well I can fix a pallid face.

I'm about ready to march over there and tell her when Uncle Charlie pats my hand. "It's going to be okay, dear heart." He stands up, commanding attention without a single word. He waits until all eyes are on him before he speaks.

"Let's all go downstairs to Dux and finish this discussion over lunch. My treat."

Bobby says he's going to tour Sun Studios, *thank you anyway*, and Fayrene says she has to report her near demise to Jarvetis, *thank you very much*.

After they leave, Mama says, "You three go ahead. I'm staying here to take my bath. Alone."

If Uncle Charlie were the type, he'd say, *Over my dead body*. Instead he replies, "I'm not leaving. Here, Lovie. Use this." He passes his credit card to her.

"Charlie Valentine," Mama says, "if you don't get out of here, I won't be responsible for what I'll do."

He shakes his head no.

"I'll stay," I volunteer reluctantly. When Mama says *alone*, that's what she means.

"Callie, you are not my keeper. Leave Elvis if you think I need a watchdog. And Lovie, get your baseball bat. If the killer comes in here, I'll make him wish he hadn't."

With her hands on her hips, she marches over and stands toe to toe with Uncle Charlie.

"Satisfied?"

"No."

"You might as well give up, Charlie. I have only one compromise in me, and that was it for today."

Mama wins and we head to Dux. It's a duck-themed restaurant (what else?) in the lobby, a bit more upscale than Mallards, but not as posh as Chez Philippe across the hall. While Lovie gets her baseball bat, Uncle Charlie and I sit in padded rattan chairs at a secluded table in the far corner studying menus which feature award-winning items she'll approve of. For one thing, they serve grilled slabs of Black Angus beef. She says it's the best, that you can tell the difference.

"Jack heard about the murders," Uncle Charlie says, and my mind flies completely off Black Angus beef. But it does linger a bit over the term *the best*, and I'm not fixing to feel guilty. "He's flying to Memphis."

I hope my face is not turning pink. Though I dread putting my willpower to the test in such a romantic old hotel, I can't say I'm sorry Jack's coming. He has a way (mostly irritating, but sometimes wonderful) of making everything seem all right.

"From where?"

"China."

"Holy cow!"

I glance toward the doorway to see if Lovie is back, but there's no sign of her. It might be a while before I ever get another opportunity like this.

"Uncle Charlie. I've been meaning to ask you. Why are you and Jack so close?".

He knows every move my almost-ex makes, and I don't believe in coincidence. I believe in destiny and fate and star-guided paths and soul mates. Well, I believe in unicorns, too, but that's a whole 'nother story.

When I ask my question, the change in Uncle Charlie is subtle. Only a niece who loves him would notice. He has gone from inviting and gentle to inscrutable and steely.

"I like Jack."

"I think there's more."

"Don't think about it, dear heart."

I reach across the table and squeeze his hands. "Please, Uncle Charlie. I need to know."

"I can't tell you."

He gently removes his hands and unfolds his napkin as carefully as if it might contain a poison-tipped knife.

I've never openly challenged Uncle Charlie, never even felt the need. But today, the need to know supersedes all else. I brace myself to butt heads with the surrogate father who apparently has secrets of his own.

"What's The Company?"

Uncle Charlie's visibly rattled, not his usual behavior at all.

"Jack told me. *Please*, Uncle Charlie."

"Let it drop, dear heart. It's best you don't know."

The things I know, even if they're bad, don't scare me nearly as much as the unknown. I can prepare for the known. But how do you brace yourself if you don't have a clue whether you're going to be hit by a tornado or swept away in a flood?

"I won't quit until I find out. Can't you see, Uncle Charlie? Because of this secrecy, my marriage is down the tubes, I'm in divorce limbo, and my chances of having a family get slimmer every day. I have to know."

He's still for a long while, and I pray he's not thinking up some literary quote to smooth things over. If he starts spouting Shakespeare, I'm going to scream.

"All right. If I didn't know you as well as I do . . ." He heaves a big sigh. "I'm counting on your strength and your intelligence. You have to promise not to ask about this again. I want you to forget you ever heard of The Company. Never mention the name again, even in private. Understood?"

I can only nod. If I open my mouth I'm afraid I'll start upchucking. I tie my napkin in knots, waiting.

"I was retiring when Jack came on board." Which means Uncle Charlie has been leading a double life for a long time. It also explains my uncle's mysterious fishing trips. "They wanted me to stay long enough to train him."

"To do what?"

"There are problems that can't be handled through the usual channels." He gives me a piercing look that causes me to shiver.

"Like what?" When my uncle doesn't answer, I start imagining Jack in the terrifying missions I've seen portrayed in movies and read about in crime thrillers. I get a sick feeling in the pit of my stomach. "You mean like secret government assassins?"

His continued silence is neither denial nor confirmation. "Uncle Charlie, please! Can't you tell me anything else?"

"Just one more thing. If a Company man gets caught, he's on his own. Do you understand?"

Only too well. We're talking deep, deep cover here, and so much danger and intrigue I don't even want to imagine what a Company man does.

Now I know why both Uncle Charlie and Jack always choose secluded corners in restaurants and why they always sit facing the door, backs to the wall. Now I know why Jack never gives me advance notice of his trips and never tells me where he's going or what he's doing.

And at long last, I know why Jack would never and *will never* consent to be a father.

I probably look like a normal person sitting in a chair in a public place. In reality, I'm a shattered-china-cup woman, holding myself together by sheer determination.

Uncle Charlie squeezes my hand. "Jack's the best. He always gets his man." There's a sense of pride in his voice. "He's going to be okay."

"After we married, why didn't he just get out?"

"That's not for me to say."

"You had a family. Why couldn't he?"

When Uncle Charlie comes around the table and wraps his arms around me, saying,"Shhh, shhh," I know I'm on the edge, drawing attention.

"I'm okay, Uncle Charlie. Really, I am." When he sits back down, I make myself take a drink of water, will myself to look at the menu until I can quit shaking inside.

"Here comes Lovie. Are you all right, dear heart?"

"Yes."

"She can't know. Nor Ruby Nell," Uncle Charlie says.

"I got it."

I almost wish I didn't. Whoever said ignorance is bliss was on the right track. Being prepared is highly overrated. Sure, you can brace yourself for natural disasters, go to storm shelters, hunker down in the basement with a week's supply of water and canned goods. Get in your car and leave, for goodness sake.

But how can you prepare to send a husband into the unknown, doing the unthinkable, and never hear from him again, never know what happened? How do you brace yourself for fifty years of watching and waiting? How would you keep fear from outstripping hope?

Lovie slides into a chair beside me, and it's like standing in front of a bracing ocean breeze.

"I got Aunt Ruby Nell all squared away with my baseball bat. Where are the drinks?" She signals a waiter. "I want my coffee with a touch of chicory—not strong, just a dollop—and plenty of cream. The real McCoy, not that imitation junk."

"We don't do imitation." The waiter drips blue-blood breeding, something he probably learned in intense haughty waiter training.

"Good. Now wiggle your cute butt. If I don't get a shot of caffeine tout de suite, you might as well go ahead and call out the paddy wagon."

She snatches up her menu and goes straight for the beef.

"Have you two ordered?"

"Not yet." Uncle Charlie has to do the talking. I still don't trust myself to speak.

"Good. I don't like anybody to get a head start on me."

The waiter appears with her coffee, then hovers while she takes a sip and pronounces it just right. Lovie and Uncle Charlie order the Angus T-bone, rare. I order a salad and wonder how I'm going to eat a bite.

"Okay," Lovie says. "Have you two solved the murder?"

"I think it's best to let Jack handle it."

"Since when?" Lovie looks at her daddy like he's gone mad. "He can't handle his libido, much less murder from afar."

Uncle Charlie says, "Now, now, dear heart," and I say, "Jack's heading this way."

"Well, hotty totty for him. I hope he's not expecting you to roll out the welcome mat. You've got bigger fish to fry."

Lovie's fond of clichés. And while she's also fond of Jack, she's not rooting for him the way Mama and Uncle Charlie are. She waits for no man, and expects me to do the same. I wish I had her ability to forget about the past and keep moving forward.

"Lovie, why don't you take Callie sightseeing this afternoon?"

I see through my uncle. He's trying to take my mind off Jack and keep us out of trouble at the same time.

"With murder afoot? Are you kidding me, Daddy?"

Uncle Charlie sighs. "All right. I know you're going to defy me. All I ask is that you stay out of trouble."

"Avoiding trouble is my middle name."

Uncle Charlie just shakes his head, hurries through his meal, then hurries off, saying he has some business to take care of before he checks on Mama—who certainly needs lots of checking on. And I don't even want to know Uncle Charlie's business, especially if it involves Jack.

Lovie refuses to rush through food and, frankly, I'm glad for the chance to sit and think. Not that I'm going to get it around my whirlwind cousin.

"Daddy always wished I was a boy."

"He loves you."

"Maybe. But he still wishes I'd been born with dangling body parts."

Lovie adds more cream to her coffee, and while she appears nonchalant, I know better. Sometimes I think most of her outrageous behavior is a bid to capture Uncle Charlie's attention. I wish she could understand that in his understated, steady way he does love her.

To give her credit, she's probably remembering his outright adoration of her mother and figuring she falls short. I know her. Maybe better than I know myself.

"I got another telegram from Rocky."

"What did he say?"

"I've been replaced by the Principal Bird Deity and the Long-lipped God."

"I doubt you've been replaced by Mayan deities,

Lovie. At least you know where he is and what he's doing."

She gives me a sharp look. "What's that all about?"

"Forget it. Let's pay the check and get out of here." I signal the waiter. "We've got to find wigs and then we've got to figure out a way to get into Mr. Whitenton's room without Mama knowing."

"Or Daddy." Lovie whips out his card, and the stiff-backed waiter marches off. "You forget, he's going to be right next door with Aunt Ruby Nell."

That complicates things. But it doesn't make them impossible. I refuse to accept defeat and I'm certainly not going to sit around and let Jack handle things.

Sure, it has been nice to have him charge to the rescue a few times, but I'm not the wilting-flower kind. I can take care of myself.

In light of what I know, I may never let Jack handle anything again. Especially my bedroom activities.

We head to the hotel's beauty salon, which, it turns out, has a pretty nice collection of wigs. While Lovie debates the merits of a black pageboy versus a bleached blond shag, I check out the competition. The chairs are filled with clients getting cut, colored, and touched up. I'm happy to report Memphis doesn't have a thing over Mooreville. In fact, I'd say Hair.Net is on the cutting edge of style and beauty.

While I'm standing there watching a botched haircut and itching to get my hands on the scissors, the "William Tell Overture" jangles and I nearly jump out of my shoes. I'm beginning to wish Lovie had brought some of her Prohibition Punch.

Fishing around in my purse, I finally find the phone. When I see the name pop up, something in my bones tells me this can't be good.

"Mama?"

She's in such a tirade, it takes me a while to sort it all out. When I do, I want to go to the back room and drown myself in the washbasin. I might as well take down my Hair.Net sign and put up one that says, "Callie Valentine Jones, Disaster Management."

I slam the phone back in my purse. "Just pick something, and fast, Lovie. I'll meet you in Mama's room."

"What's wrong?"

"She's nearly killed Thomas and she says she's fixing to kill Uncle Charlie."

Elvis' Opinion #6 on Bathtubs, Baseball Bats, and Bravery

The situation in Ruby Nell's room is not pretty, but I'm on top of it. Listen, if it hadn't been for me, the killer would have iced her this time. Drowned Ruby Nell in her Calgon bubble bath.

There I was, minding my own business . . . Well, sulking, if you want to know the truth. I'm sick and tired of being cooped up in this room when Memphis is waiting to bow at my paws.

This is the town where I made my mark, went from truck driver to overnight sensation, bought my first pink Cadillac, made pink my signature color. Don't tell me fans aren't lurking behind closed doors playing "Love Me Tender" and hoping for the day I reappear. I've swapped my jumpsuit for a dog suit, but I can still bring fans to a screaming frenzy.

All I have to do is walk into Lansky's Gift Shop downstairs and you'd see some adulation. They'd know how to treat the man who put the Lansky name on the map. (Bernard was my clothier.)

But I digress. Back to the mayhem on the tenth floor. There Ruby Nell was, up to her neck in bubbles while I lolled around on her bed keeping an eye peeled on the door. (Actually, I was hoping a housekeeper might come in and I could make my escape.)

Things were getting pretty boring and I was about to doze off when my mismatched ears saved us all.

I heard the killer coming—stealthy footsteps, the key turning in the lock. (Yeah, he had a key. Bet nobody else knows that.) Next, my nose kicked in. You'd have to look long and hard to find a better nose than a hound has. Just about any hound will do but, of course, I'm prejudiced. Bassets are the best.

Trey would argue for redbone hounds, but I'd win. I always do. He hasn't yet learned it's useless to match wits against a dog who once brought the world to its knees with a smoky Southern gospel and blues voice and a pair of sexy hips that wouldn't stay still.

Anyhow, I leaped off the bed and started a howling rendition of "Jailhouse Rock." Ruby Nell yelled, "What's going on out there, Elvis?" and I segued into "Only the Strong Survive."

About the time she burst out of the bathroom, naked as a boiled egg, wielding Lovie's baseball bat, Thomas galloped through the connecting door like an over-the-hill racehorse, his skinny legs pumping three feet in the air. (Take it from me. Men built like Thomas Whitenton should never be seen in public wearing nothing but shorts and socks.)

Lovie's bat connected with skinny, hairy thighs and amidst the commotion, the real killer ran toward the front door.

Naturally I was hot on his trail, howling "That's All Right, Mama" so Ruby Nell would know I had the situation under control. I was just fixing to take a bite out of crime when Charlie barreled in and got between me and my goal.

Ordinarily he'd have noticed the killer slithering behind the door, but all he could see was Mr. Whitenton in his Fruit of the Looms. Before Thomas could hum "I Beg of You," Charlie waded in with fists flying while the real assailant slipped out the door.

You don't want to hear the gory details. Suffice it to say, Charlie Valentine could still register his hands as lethal weapons.

Ruby Nell was yelling her head off that he had the wrong man, but Charlie didn't hear her till she picked up Lovie's bat and threatened bodily harm if he didn't stop.

I sashayed around trying to smooth things over so Callie wouldn't have to deal with it, but Ruby Nell called her anyway. To top it off, Fayrene and Bobby fluttered in and began flouncing around.

This room looks like a three-ring Barnum and Bailey circus. There's nothing I can do now except wait for my human mom. My stalwart presence and reassuring manner will hold her together. That will have to do till I can get her back home and sit on her lap in the front porch swing and help her fall into the soothing rhythms of my beating heart.

Chapter 13

Suspects, Motives, and Music Gate Madness

I arrive at Mama's room at the same time as the Memphis Police Department. By now I'm on a first name basis with the one I privately call Baby Face. When he says, "You again," I just shrug.

"What can I say? 'I love this dinky town.'"

He looks at me like I've gone crazy. Obviously he never saw Burt Lancaster in *Sweet Smell of Success*. I flash a big smile I don't feel and he leaves me alone to seek out somebody sane. Translated: Uncle Charlie over by the window, obviously in charge.

What was I going to do? Lie down and cry? Throw a pity party and invite myself to be the guest of honor? Though I feel like doing all those things, that's not my style.

Elvis rubs against my legs and I lean down for some contact with reality. When you're running into dead bodies and attempted murder everywhere you turn, it feels good to ground yourself with a dog. Their rules are simple: eat, sleep, roll in the grass, wag your tail, wait for treats.

While I pet Elvis, I survey the scene. Fayrene, Bobby, and Mama are hovered around the bed. I ease over to the left to see what the attraction is. Wouldn't you know it's Mr. Whitenton? He's lying there with a sheet draped haphazardly over his skinny bones, moaning and carrying on like he's dying. From the look of things, he's not wearing many clothes.

This is more of Thomas Whitenton than I ever wanted to know. I can't look away fast enough. Glancing across the room, I check the connecting door. Just as I suspected: it's wide open.

Mama's rubbing his face with a wet washcloth, but when she sees me she abandons him (thank goodness, and I don't say that to be mean). She rushes over, purple caftan flying and Fayrene riding her tailwinds.

"Mama, what happened?"

"The killer got in here, that's what. If it hadn't been for Elvis, I'd be dead."

"Did you see him?"

"No. He was wearing a mask."

"What kind of mask, Mama?"

"Woody Woodpecker."

A strange choice for a killer, but when you consider the power of a woodpecker's beak and the strength it took to heave Babs over the balustrade and the Amazonian Gloria into the fountain, maybe the mask is symbolic.

"If this keeps on," Fayrene says, "he's going to get one of us."

When she gets home, she'll retell the story at

Gas, Grits, and Guts with so many embellishments, she and Mama will become legend.

"If he was wearing a mask, how do you know it was a man?"

I think it was the man lying on the bed, but I want confirmation from Mama that I'm on the right track.

"Because I heard him speak."

"What did he say?"

" 'Die, hoochie mama.' "

I have to sit down. Until now I wanted to believe that Mr. Whitenton wouldn't really kill Mama. Or that she exaggerated the attacks to put herself at the center of the drama playing out at the Peabody.

Lovie sweeps in with a bag from the beauty shop, takes one look, and strides over to me. "What are you doing on the floor?"

"Resting." I reach for her hand. "Help me up."

"What's going on here, Aunt Ruby Nell?"

"I know who the killer is."

"You didn't tell me that, Mama."

"I was waiting for you to get off the floor."

"Well?" Sometimes Mama carries her dramatic pauses too far. "Who is it?"

"I don't know his name, but he speaks with a lisp. He actually said, 'hoothie mama.' "

"Do the police and Uncle Charlie know?"

"Do I look like I was born yesterday?" She motions to Fayrene. "Come on, we've got to get Thomas to a doctor."

Uncle Charlie blocks Mama's headlong rush to the afflicted. "The police have taken care of that, Ruby Nell. Paramedics are on the way."

As if he's choreographed their moves, the cops

file by with their notepads and badges and guns. And paramedics rush in to haul Mr. Whitenton off on a gurney.

Even with Fayrene and Bobby still here, there's suddenly room to breathe. Uncle Charlie marches over to lock the connecting door while the rest of us mill around like prisoners seeing daylight for the first time in six years. We all find seats, then just sit there, breathing. I nearly topple over asleep.

"From now on, Ruby Nell, that door stays locked."

"On one condition, Charlie. You deprived me of my dance partner. You take his place."

"I don't dance anymore. Besides, you're the one who broke his leg with a baseball bat."

"That's the deal, Charlie. Take it or leave it."

Mama and Uncle Charlie are both strong-willed people accustomed to winning. I don't know whether to referee, pray, or run.

Finally Uncle Charlie speaks. "Done."

Lovie and I stare at each other. What is going on here? The relationship between Mama and Uncle Charlie has shifted so many times in the last few hours, I feel as if I'm at the Mississippi–Alabama Fair and Dairy Show, riding an out-of-control tilt-a-whirl. From the way Lovie's mouth is hanging open, I'd say she feels the same way.

"Now." Uncle Charlie puts his hands in his pockets, looking almost jovial. "There's a special dancers' tour of Graceland leaving from the hotel in thirty minutes. We're all going."

"I'm staying here. I want to run to the hospital and check on Thomas." Mama sashays to the bathroom and shuts herself in. Uncle Charlie marches over and doesn't even bother to knock.

"We're all going, Ruby Nell. Especially you. And that's final." His commanding voice carries through the door.

I don't hear what Mama says, but it makes Uncle Charlie chuckle and that's good enough for me.

Everybody agrees to meet in the lobby in thirty minutes, and Lovie and I hurry toward the elevator. We need to regroup and, frankly, I could use a bath. A nap, too, but that's out of the question.

"Daddy's planning to keep an eye on all of us."

"I agree, Lovie. He told me to stay out of the investigation."

"You're not going to let Daddy tell you what to do, are you?"

I punch the elevator button, then watch the floor numbers light up. If I keep racing between floors four and ten, I'm going to need my own private elevator.

"Maybe he's right, Lovie. You could put everything we know about solving crime in a teacup."

She says a word that stops clocks. "We are *not* giving up. We'll just have to figure a way to get into Thomas' room without Daddy knowing."

The elevator stops and two women get off, leaving their fragrances behind. I'm getting ready to ask Lovie if she thinks the killer's lisp is real or fake when she sidesteps and I spot the duck master, standing at the back in a bowler hat. He might have looked dashing if he'd been wearing something besides blue jeans and a windbreaker, but at least he's trying.

Lovie and I clam up. No sense talking murder in front of strangers. The duck master spots Elvis and puts his handkerchief over his face.

"Are you allergic to dogs?" I hope he's not, poor man.

He fans his hands in front of his face. "Dog germs."

I revise my opinion. If I could bench press Elvis, I'd lift him over my head so his thumping tail would knock that silly hat off.

The duck master reaches over and punches the eighth-floor button, though clearly he was headed to the lobby. I can't say I'm sorry to see him go. People who say ugly things about animals don't deserve a nonstop ride. When Elvis growls as he departs, it's just icing on my cake.

When we get to our room, I head straight to the bathroom.

"Lovie, I have to take a bath, no matter what. If I'm not out in fifteen minutes, knock."

Her cell phone is ringing and she motions me to go ahead. I'd love to fill the tub with bubbles, light candles, put on music, pour a big glass of Lovie's Prohibition Punch, and spend the next hour in bathtub heaven. For one thing, I don't have time. Too, I'd either fall asleep in the tub or start remembering my last long scented soak at the Peabody.

With Jack. Our anniversary. Two years ago. We had the honeymoon suite. Bubbles up to our necks. Candles galore. Buttered lobster, key lime pie, champagne.

A leisurely bath would even remind me of the date I cancelled with Champ because of a summer cold. He came anyway, drew me a hot bath, made chicken soup and hot tea, then later sat on the sofa holding my hand while I leaned against his shoulder. It would have been a lovely, homey evening if Jack hadn't shown up with some old Western DVDs. The three of us spent the rest of the evening watching John Wayne.

No, when I'm feeling vulnerable, it's best not to luxuriate in the bath and wax nostalgic.

Turning the water on full blast, I step in and drench myself, hair and all. Luckily my hair will fall back into place whether I blow-dry it or let it air dry. I can even sleek it with gel and go with the wet-head, sophisticated look.

Feeling like a better person, I emerge and find Lovie jiving around the room.

"Practicing for tomorrow's jitterbug competition?"

"No. I'm not going to compete against Daddy. Besides, I don't need to goad Rocky anymore. He's invited me to Mexico."

She swing dances around the room singing "La Cucaracha." I can picture her swooping through the jungle, sending cockroaches and every other living thing running, captivating everybody she sees. Especially Rocky. Oh, I do hope she captivates the only man who has ever realized she's a treasure.

"I'm so happy for you, Lovie."

"You can come, too. Rocky won't mind."

See, that's what I mean. Generous hearted to a fault. They don't make Lovies anymore.

"Thanks, but I think three would ruin the effect of moonlight over Mayan ruins." I finish dressing, then grab my purse and Elvis' leash. "We'd better hurry."

* * *

Uncle Charlie and Mama are waiting for us. Bobby had errands and Fayrene decided to wait at the hotel for Jarvetis. Apparently their fight over the séance room at Gas, Grits, and Guts is over. According to Mama, "Jarvetis came to his senses when he realized he nearly lost Fayrene."

Uncle Charlie leads us to the back of the bus (naturally, so he can sit with his back to the wall) and I study everybody who gets on. When Victor enters with his wife, I punch Lovie. I wonder if Victor knows his wife was consorting with Grayson Mims.

If we can escape Uncle Charlie's watchful eye, we might get a chance to do some sleuthing.

Right behind the Mabrys is the woman with the polecat hair we saw this morning on Beale Street. And she's heading this way. I nudge Lovie, who gives me a dark look.

"I'm not blind."

"You're hissing, Lovie."

"Stop punching and I'll stop hissing."

"*Okay.*"

Polecat hair stands in the aisle and asks the gentleman in front of us, "Is this seat taken?" He shakes his head and she slides in, then extends her hand. "I'm Carolyn Mims."

Mims? Grayson's ex-wife? Sister? Sister-in-law? That rules out "lover," as in, *Grayson and his lover conspired to kill his wife, Babs.* As soon as Lovie and I can find a private spot, we'll have to discuss what to do about this new twist.

The bus heads south on I-55 and within minutes we're in the parking lot on Elvis Presley Boulevard across from the Music Gates of Graceland. Fans are already pouring through and up the driveway to the mansion that was Elvis' Tennessee home. It should be easy to get lost in this crowd.

All the dancers (I use the term loosely, because all of these people are amateurs and many are Mama's age, to boot) pile off the bus and pour into a 1970s-era airport terminal to see Elvis' private custom jets. All, that is, except Victor and his Barbie-doll wife. They're heading toward the Music Gates.

I think up the only excuse Uncle Charlie will buy. "I'll catch up later. I have to go to the bathroom."

I scoop up Elvis, give Lovie the look, and she trots along beside me.

"This is not the way to the bathroom," she says, "so where are we headed?"

"Tailing suspects."

I nod toward Victor and Stepford wife number two, who is color-coordinated from the pink rhinestone-studded headband in her super-coiffed, over-sprayed blond pageboy to the cute pair of pink wedge heels on her tiny feet.

They start fighting the minute they're clear of the rest of the tour group. I step up my pace.

"Hurry, Lovie."

From the body language and the sound of angry voices, it looks as if one of the Mabrys is going to be the next victim.

Chapter 14

Jilting, Jiving, and Jail

We race across the street trying to look as if we're here to see the Meditation Garden instead of what the Mabrys are up to. Trouble, it looks like.

It's one of those beautiful, still October days when conversations float around like kites, landing in the hands (and ears) of the unintended.

"But Carolyn *caught* you coming out of his room, Jill."

Carolyn? Mims? The room Victor's talking about is obviously Grayson's because we caught her going in. This has suddenly become a don't-miss, murder-connected conversation.

"I was just being sympathetic, Victor."

"Bull."

"What if I wasn't? You have no right to judge. You'd still be carrying a torch for Babs if she weren't dead."

Victor retreats into screaming silence.

Was Jill jealous of Babs because Victor still loved

her? Or was she jealous because Babs had Grayson and she wanted him? Either way, this little picture-postcard wife has a powerful motive for the first murder.

But what's her connection to victims number two and three?

Victor shakes himself like a man coming out of a bad dream.

"Leave Babs out of this."

"You wish. You never got over her jilting you for Grayson."

Jill flounces through the Music Gates and Victor stops right in our path. I almost plow into him, and Lovie *does*.

"Watch where you're going," he yells.

He calls Lovie a name that won't do to repeat. For a minute, I think she's fixing to jerk him up, throw him on the ground, and step on him. She's capable.

And if she doesn't, I'm so mad, I'm liable to do it myself.

"Chill out, buster," Lovie says.

When we walk around him, I notice she squashes Victor's foot with the steel-reinforced heel of her cowboy boot. Deliberately. Lovie's anything but clumsy.

I give her a high five and we hotfoot it up the winding driveway toward the mansion. With its vaulting Corinthian columns and soft buff-colored brick, Graceland is the epitome of the Old South. You expect to see women in hoop skirts and gentlemen with mint juleps strolling around the lawn.

White wrought-iron benches, white lions on low

brick columns, and large white urns planted with impatiens flank the front steps. Boxwood hedges are clipped into meatball shapes and the lawn is laid out with flowerbeds in geometrical Italian garden design. The perfect symmetry outside this mansion is greatly at odds with the man who vaulted to stardom by defying all convention.

The minute I put Elvis down, he heists his leg on a stone lion and looks primed to anoint the other. But Jill is getting away.

"Not now, boy."

Ahead of us, Jill darts around the house. Lovie races off but I scurry to keep up without upsetting Elvis, who likes to amble. They're heading toward the sign that says, PUBLIC RESTROOMS. A boon for me. I shine in public toilets, especially in the Deep South where women have a habit of going in to do business and refresh their lipstick, then end up spilling their life stories to rank strangers.

I'm the rank stranger they usually pick. Lovie says it's because I'm a sucker for sob stories, but I think it's because I've put a welcome mat instead of a keep out sign on my personal space. Besides, I like to help people.

I arrive at the restroom right behind Lovie. At first glance, it appears empty. Then I see the cute pair of wedge heels under the stall door.

If you ask me, that's a strike in Jill's favor. Women interested in cute shoes aren't usually the murdering kind. Unless you count the peroxided, flat-chested teenage wannabe who tried to mow me down at last year's Labor Day sale.

I motion to Lovie, who glances at Jill's shoes,

then heads into the adjacent stall. I'm afraid of losing Jill, and besides, I don't have to pee, so I sidle over to the sinks and wash my hands, one eye peeled toward the pink shoes.

For a while, there's nothing but the sound of running water. When Lovie comes out, Jill is still holed up inside. Not a single sound filters through.

"Do you think she's dead?" I whisper.

Lovie squares her shoulders and sticks out her chin. I know this look. She's getting ready to charge through the stall door to the rescue.

"Wait." I grab hold of her sleeve.

A loud wailing spills from the stall and both tiny pink-clad feet collapse sideways. From this view, Jill's feet look like those of a dejected child who just dropped her ice cream cone.

"Are you all right?" I ask.

The wailing gets louder. Maybe I should have kept my mouth shut, waited for her to come out. It's too late for hindsight now. I knock on Jill's stall door.

"Can I help you? Are you okay?"

"I'm . . ." Jill's words get swallowed up by more intense sobbing. It wouldn't be polite to jerk open the door. I knock again.

"Do you need assistance? Can I call somebody?"

Finally the sobbing subsides and I hear a big hiccup. Fishing a pretty lace-edged handkerchief from my purse, I pass it over the door.

"Here, this might help."

"Thank you."

I revise my opinion about Jill Mabry. Anybody that polite didn't kill Babs Mabry Mims.

Jill snorts into the handkerchief, then hiccups again. "Nothing can help. It's all ruined."

"Maybe it's not as bad as you think. Just give it time."

Lovie rolls her eyes. But I'm good at giving advice, and she knows it. Why else would I have people—all with stories to tell—flocking from six counties to get appointments at Hair.Net? I mean, besides the fact that I'm a top-notch stylist?

Soft snuffling sounds come from the other side of the door. I tap lightly.

"Do you want to talk about it?"

There's a big silence and the little pink shoes under the door shift sideways. I can picture Jill changing to a more comfortable position on the toilet seat.

I'm about to give up when she says, "My husband was in love with a dead woman." She sniffs again. "Well, she wasn't dead till we got here, but still . . . Now she's perfect, the immortal dead."

I get shivers. Did Victor kill his first wife because he couldn't have her, and then accuse Grayson as revenge for stealing her?

"Maybe you just thought your husband was in love with her," I say.

"No. He called her two or three times a day."

Lovie opens her mouth, but I motion her to be quiet. Another voice might scare Jill off.

Apparently Jill interprets my silence for disbelief.

"I checked his cell phone."

She has the shamed voice of a little girl who lied

about how many Girl Scout cookies she sold. My mothering instincts race to the forefront.

"That's okay. Under certain circumstances, a woman has to do whatever it takes."

Jill surprises me by giggling. "The devil made me do it."

"What did you do?"

"I slept with Grayson Mims."

Her confession shocks even Lovie. I can tell she's thinking the same thing I am. If Grayson slept with another woman the day after his wife's murder, then he's right back at the top of the suspect list.

"Well, not really, but almost. I just meant to comfort him and I guess he thought I was leading him on." Jill starts crying again. "And now they both hate meeeeeee."

I assume she's talking about Victor and Grayson. We wait for the crying to stop, but she's on a jag.

"Is she going to stay in there all day?" Lovie whispers.

"Shhh. She'll hear."

Sure enough, Jill says, "Is somebody out there besides you?"

"Yes, my best friend. But you can trust her absolutely. One hundred percent."

Jill is so quiet I wonder if Lovie has blown it. And I wanted to find out if Jill knows polecat hair and what her connection is to the other two victims.

"I have an idea," Lovie says. "Why don't you come out of the stall and tour around Graceland with us? There's nothing like three sassy women swinging into the Jungle Room."

"Really? You'd let me tag along?"

"Tag along, my big fat attitude." I'll grant you, Lovie has plenty of that. "We'll roar into the Jungle Room like the wildest cats in the jungle."

The door swings open and Jill emerges, mascara streaked to her chin and eyes puffy.

"Wait." She stares at me. "Don't I know you?"

Holy cow. She remembers me from Grayson's room, impersonating a housekeeper.

"Probably."

I take her arm and lead her toward the bank of washbasins. She hands me the wadded up, wilted-looking handkerchief.

"Just keep it." I turn on the water. "We're here with Mama for the dance competition. And this is my dog, Elvis." He prances over and licks her ankles. He's a sucker for pretty women. "We were the ones making all the ruckus in the lobby early this morning."

"Oh, Lord, he's so *cuuuute*."

Elvis is lapping up the attention. The ham.

My cell phone rings, causing all of us to jump. Lovie takes over with Jill while I answer.

"Where are you?"

It's Mama, checking up. Not that I mind. Sometimes it's inconvenient, but mostly it's comforting. It means there's one person in the world who loves me enough to want to know my whereabouts at all times. Granted, she's a bit nosey, too, but love far outweighs that.

"Lovie and I decided to skip the planes and cars.

We're on the grounds, getting ready to check out the mansion."

"That poor old Carolyn Mims is following us around like a lost chicken and Charlie's driving me crazy. He won't let me out of sight. I can't even go to the bathroom."

"Hang in there, Mama. You're more than his match."

Mama loves flattery. Satisfied, she hangs up. With my mind eased over Mama's safety, I can continue mining this goldfield named Jill Mabry.

It's remarkable what a splash of water and a little lipstick can do for the young. You'd never know Jill had been crying.

She's been hurt enough today. I hope she doesn't suspect Lovie and I have ulterior motives for our kindness. Though, to tell the truth, we'd have done it anyway. Nothing bonds women like a good cry and some timely sympathy.

The three of us link arms and head out the restroom door like lifelong friends. That's one of the things I love about women. You can form these fast bonds in less time than it takes most folks to order a McDonald's hamburger.

I stay away from the subject of murder, and Lovie follows my lead. It's best to let Jill get comfortable with us, laugh a bit, give her time to let down her guard.

By the time we enter the mansion, she's beginning to relax. She stands in front of the twin stained-glass panels in Elvis' living room admiring the opulent colors of the peacocks' tails.

"I just love peacocks," she says.

"I have a dress that shade of blue-green," Lovie tells her.

"Oh, that must be lovely with your beautiful blue eyes."

See what I mean about Jill? A woman that generous hearted couldn't possibly be a killer.

I linger in front of the panels, watching the stream of tourists for a glimpse of polecat hair. I guess I ought to think of her as Carolyn now that I know her name, but first impressions are hard to shake.

Too, I'm giving the other tourists time to move to other parts of the house. If you let other people hear your private conversations, they'll come up with all sorts of silly surmises.

Last summer, Mabel Moffett heard me asking for an early-pregnancy testing kit in Walgreens and it got out all over Mooreville that I was pregnant—and they didn't know who the father was since Jack had moved out.

When Mama heard the rumors she got so mad she told everybody the kit was for her. Furthermore, she said it in such a way that nobody dared laugh.

See what I'm talking about? Love like that is worth the little bit of aggravation.

There's no sign of the mysterious Mims woman, so I give Lovie the signal and we both herd Jill toward the Jungle Room. She's moving along with a swing in her steps—a tribute to the resilience of youth—when Victor bursts through the front door.

He immediately spots his wife and storms our way. This can't be good. Jill goes pale, ducks behind Lovie.

"Jill, what do you think you're doing?"

Victor's so mad he's speaking through gritted teeth. He looks angry enough to hit something—probably Lovie.

When he grabs for his wife, Lovie spreads her arms wide and blocks his move.

"Try that again, hotshot, and you're going to draw back a nub."

"That's my wife. And she's coming with me."

Jill peers around Lovie. "Go away, Victor. I'm not coming with you."

For a horrible minute I think Lovie and I are going to be in the center of a marital brawl in Graceland. We'll be headline news. Our pictures will be splashed on every paper in the country. (From behind bars.)

Much to my relief, Victor shrugs and stomps off. Then this little-girl-lost voice comes from behind Lovie.

"I can't stay with that man tonight. What am I going to do?"

I put my arm around her. "You'll stay with us, of course."

Lovie gives me our secret-signal look, but I ignore her. What does she expect me to do? Leave this poor, stray kitten in the room with a man who might have killed his first wife and apparently is now bent on killing his second?

Elvis' Opinion #7 on Pink Cadillacs, Pecan Pie, and Bleeding Hearts

I could have told you my human mom would pick up this stray babe-in-the-woods. Callie's a true bleeding heart. The next thing you know, she'll be decorating one of the spare rooms of my Mooreville house in Pepto-Bismol pink and trying to adopt Jill Mabry.

At least I'd have somebody else in the house partial to pink. Listen, if I can seize the opportunity to sneak off, I'm liable to hot-wire my 1955 pink Cadillac and go joyriding through the streets of Memphis. It would feel good to have my ears blowing in the wind and everybody screaming, "Elvis! Elvis!" I might even mosey over to Sun Studios and cut another record. Wouldn't that make headline news!

"Elvis lives" rumors have been floating around for years.

You're doggone tootin', he lives. Everybody around Mooreville knows it, but I'd like to let the rest of the world in on the secret.

I've been working on this song. Well, my human daddy and I have been working on it together. Still, I'm the one with the pipes to turn it into a hit. It's called "Cats Can't Wear Blue Suede Shoes." Jack has another name for it, but what does he know about the music business?

I know every in and out. Besides that, I can hear a song one time, then sing it word for word in perfect pitch. That used to amaze folks. Of course, the thing that really amazed them was my voice.

Let me tell you, I can still command the attention of every tomcat that tries to sneak under Callie's back fence. When I roar through the doggie door and howl "Separate Ways," they know I mean business.

Lovie and Callie and this Jill kitten are passing by my kitchen now without so much as a glance. I hang back, hoping Callie will let me stroll in, sit down at the table, and wait for a big old piece of hot pecan pie. Vanilla ice cream on top. I used to come down here in the middle of the night when I couldn't wind down from a big show. It was quiet, and I could hear the music in my head without everybody fussing over me and the Colonel telling me what to do.

And there was always plenty of good country cooking in the Graceland kitchen. Meatloaf, black-eyed peas, fried green tomatoes.

Callie tugs my leash, but not hard. Considering some of the human moms I might have had, I'm one lucky dog.

Obviously, though, she doesn't hear what I hear. Grayson and Carolyn Mims holed up together in the doorway down the hall. He wasn't on the bus, which means he knew where Carolyn was and came looking for her.

They're arguing about none other than the little stray Jilly kitten Callie's adopted.

"Good lord, Grayson, didn't you think having a sleazy fling with Jill Mabry might implicate you?"

"I've told you. We didn't do anything. I was distraught and she was sweet. And available."

"She's *not* available, you idiot. If you had to find comfort in the arms of another woman, why didn't you pick somebody not wearing a ring? That voluptuous redhead from Mississippi."

Lovie'd get a kick out of that. She'd probably use it to goad poor old Rocky.

"I didn't *pick* anybody, Carolyn. How many times do I have to tell you? I was in Mallards crying in my beer and she was kind and we ended up in my room. That's all."

"See that it doesn't happen again."

Callie tugs me out of earshot, which might have sent me into a snit if it weren't for the Jungle Room. Coming in here always did lift my spirits. The sound of the waterfall. My big old leather chair. All that fun jungle stuff around. It makes me feel like that other king, Tarzan.

I always did have a love of whimsy and that includes comic-book characters. Listen, where do you think I got the idea for those jumpsuits I used to wear? When I was a young pup, Captain Marvel was one of my personal heroes. If you want to know the truth, he still is. And what's wrong with that? If you ask me, this world would be better off if everybody would discover the little kid inside and let him out to play.

Chapter 15

Come-to-Jesus Meeting, Miss Paris, and the Jade Belly

We don't catch up with Mama and Uncle Charlie until we board the bus. I introduce Jill, and they take this unexpected guest in stride.

She is immediately charmed with them. And why not? My uncle is the perfect Southern gentleman, and Mama can be a world-class ambassador when she tries.

"Can you join us tonight for ribs at the Rendezvous?" Uncle Charlie asks Jill.

"Thank you. I will."

Tonight is open night, which means the dancers are free to practice for tomorrow's finals. The dance floor in the Peabody's lovely Venetian Room is the designated practice area. It might be worth checking out to see if I can learn anything that will break this case. If I can get up enough energy.

I collapse into my seat and scan the boarding passengers for Victor, bracing myself to deal with him again. Oddly, he's not on the bus.

Neither is polecat hair, a.k.a Carolyn Mims. Who knows what they're up to? Maybe Jill knows something about the mysterious Carolyn, especially after getting cozy with Grayson.

Now is not the time to ask, though. I lean my head against the back of my seat and the next thing I know, Lovie is saying, "Wake up. We're here."

I shake my head to get the cotton out. For once, I'm grateful to lag and let somebody else take charge. Still groggy, I let Lovie herd me into the lobby.

Fayrene jumps out at us, shouting, "Lord, I'm all agag."

I'm agog, too, and jolted awake. In neon green with bright pink flowers, she looks like a fuchsia plant bursting over the pot. Of course, I mean that in the best way. I hang fuchsia on my porch every summer.

"What's wrong, Fayrene?" Mama asks. "Where's Jarvetis?"

"He had car trouble in Holly Springs, but he'll be here any minute. I'm so excited, I'm liable to make a pubic display."

I hope she means public, but the state she's in, I can't be certain.

"Fayrene, I want you to meet Jill," I say, and after the introductions, Mama asks if Fayrene has any news from Mr. Whitenton.

"He's back in his room, chock full of pain killers."

"Is his leg broken?"

"Don't worry, Ruby Nell. You just bruised and battered him."

Uncle Charlie listens to all this, poker faced. You can never tell what he's thinking unless he wants you to.

The three of them head to Mallards to wait for Jarvetis, while the rest of the motley crew board the elevator. Thank goodness, it's empty. I lean against the wall, and even Elvis seems tuckered out. Serves him right for getting me up in the middle of the night.

When Jill gets off on the third floor to retrieve her belongings, Lovie hands her a key to our room and offers to go with her.

"Thank you, but no. If Victor tries anything, I'll punch his lights out." Jill pumps her fist into the air, laughing.

It looks like this little kitten has claws.

"You go, girl," Lovie tells her.

The way Jill swishes out, you'd never know she was the same woman who sobbed her story to strangers in the public restroom at Graceland. That's the beauty of female friendships. Girl power. Go-get-'em-tiger attitude. Laughter. Most of all, the laughter.

"I like her, Callie."

"So do I. I've removed her from the suspect list."

"I have a great idea. I'll steal a maid's uniform for her, then I can ride the cleaning cart and she can push."

"Hush, Lovie. I'm too tired to laugh."

The elevator deposits us on the fourth floor. Lovie retrieves the *Commercial Appeal* halfway under our door, and Elvis makes a beeline for his pillow. No wonder. He's used to snoozing off and on all day.

I spot the purloined purse, jerk it up, and throw it in a drawer. And while I'm at it, I clean out a drawer for Jill. She seems like a wonderful woman, but who knows what she'd do if she recognized Babs' purse. I'm not planning to find out, and I'm certainly not ready to confess that I was the maid who saw her in Grayson's room.

Lovie's standing there with her hands on her hips, watching me.

"What?" I'm too tired to read body language.

"I wondered what you were thinking, inviting her here. With Thomas in his bed and Jill in ours, how are we going to get into his room? Not to mention the latest victim's."

"Maybe the Memphis PD will catch the killer. Shoot, maybe Jack will. If he ever gets here."

Lovie lounges in the corner chair with the paper while I kick off my shoes, plop on the bed, and pray I'm back home before the plane from China arrives. I can't deal with Jack right now, especially after what Uncle Charlie told me about The Company.

"Besides, Lovie. 'Tomorrow is another day.' "

"Thank you, Miss Scarlett."

Sometimes I wonder if Lovie and I are turning into Uncle Charlie, a quote for every occasion—though he sticks to lofty literature by Shakespeare and Emily Dickinson while we go with *Gone with the Wind* and film noir. I could do Shakespeare if I wanted, but I'm too tired to be lofty.

I'm just drifting off when Lovie's shout jerks me upright.

"What? What?"

"Listen to this. 'Local former exotic dancer, Fifi Galant, is preparing for the wedding of the season at the Peabody Hotel.' "

"You woke me to talk about a wedding?"

Ignoring me, Lovie keeps reading. " 'Ms. Galant has performed exotic dances at various clubs in Memphis including the Jade Belly . . .' "

"Holy cow, Lovie. What does that have to do with anything?"

"Wait. I'm coming to the best part. 'Fifi says she got her start at Hot Tips in Las Vegas.' Hot Tips, Cal. I wonder if she was there when I made my debut."

Trust Lovie to call her one and only performance a debut. Forget that we were in Hot Tips under deep cover. Except that Lovie's feathered costume barely even covered Christmas.

"Even if she was, Lovie, I don't see how Fifi Galant has a single thing to do with *anything*."

"Maybe she does and maybe she doesn't. Remember that stage makeup we found in Gloria's room? What if there's a connection between Fifi and Gloria? Maybe Latoya, too, since she and Gloria were friends."

I groan and punch my pillow, but Lovie's on a roll.

"Besides, her wedding is at the Peabody. That's two connections, Cal. You know there's no such thing as coincidence."

I can see there will be no catnap for me. Besides Lovie's insistence on discussing the wedding of somebody I never heard of and don't want to know, something is niggling at me. Something I can't quite put my finger on.

"If you're right, every clue we've uncovered could lead us to a dead end. The killer could be somebody not even connected to this hotel or the dance competition."

"Exactly."

"If that's true, we'd have to cover all of Memphis and Shelby County to find the killer."

The lock clicks and we both shut up. Jill puts the night latch against the door frame to keep the door open, then fills her arms with bags from the hall and backs into the room.

"Ta-da! I'm back." Her cheeks are flushed and she looks like she just won a Maytag washer and dryer.

I leap up, feeling guilty. I don't know why. Maybe it's a Southern hospitality thing—the hostess caught wallowing in the guest's bed.

"Here. This bed is yours, and I've cleaned out a drawer for your things."

"How'd it go?" Lovie says.

"Victor was there. We had a come-to-Jesus meeting."

Lovie and I don't have to ask what that is. Anybody born in the Bible Belt knows. Serious business is afoot, and the choice you make rewards you with glory or dooms you to becoming pit barbecue for Old Scratch himself.

"I told Victor in no uncertain terms I'm leaving him."

Jill kicks her tiny pink shoes onto the floor and curls up in the middle of her bed with her legs tucked, yoga style. Lovie digs into our snack stash and comes up with chips and Hershey's chocolate, and we settle in for a let-down-your-hair girl session.

It turns out Jill had high ambitions before she met Victor. She had just been crowned Miss Paris (Tennessee, not France) and planned to use the scholarship money to study medicine. Then Victor came along, freshly jilted and tragically romantic. He took one look and rushed her to the altar.

"Little did I know I'd be competing with *three* girlfriends *and* his ex-wife. And it will get worse now that Babs has become a dead saint."

She's only halfway kidding. The Valentine family sees this phenomenon almost every day: the bereaved marching into the funeral home, sanctifying the dead.

"You should go back to school, get your medical degree," I tell her. "It's never too late."

"That's exactly what I plan to do. And use a big old fat divorce settlement to pay for it."

I pride myself on being a wonderful judge of character. If Jill's a killer, I'm Shamu the whale. Emboldened by Jill's frankness, I plunge right into the subject of murder.

"Do you think Grayson killed Babs?"

"He certainly had reason. He told me she was spending him into the poorhouse and I know from the things Victor has said that Grayson was insanely jealous of him and anybody else who looked at Babs. If you can believe my idiot husband."

Jill takes off her headband and tries to shake out her hair, but she's wearing too much hairspray. When I finish finding out what she knows about murder, I'm giving her some hair advice. In a constructive way, of course.

"But I wouldn't have gone to his room," she adds, "if I thought he was the killer."

"What about that other Mims woman?" Lovie asks. "Who is she and why did she show up out of the blue?"

"Carolyn? That's Grayson's sister."

"Did she have any reason to hate Babs?" I figure anybody with hair that bad is bound to have other horrible qualities, even if it's just poor fashion taste.

"I don't know her that well, but I do remember one thing. Last Christmas, Babs had the balls to call my house. I picked up the extension and overheard her telling Victor she'd finally cut 'that rotten lowlife sister' out of Grayson's life and convinced him to take her to New York for the holidays."

Jill nibbles a piece of chocolate the size of a black-eyed pea. All that discipline, I can see why she was Miss Paris.

"Quite frankly," she adds, "Babs is the one who gives me the creeps. I might have killed her myself if somebody else hadn't beat me to it."

Lovie and I exchange a look and Jill says, "Just kidding."

Holy cow! What have I gotten us into? If I'm wrong about Jill, we're liable to wake up dead.

"If you don't mind, I need to take a bath before dinner."

She hops off the bed and hugs me, then Lovie.

"I can't thank you enough. You've given me the courage to follow through this time. And I promise I'll only be here just one night."

"You're welcome to stay as long as you like," I tell her.

"I'm going home tomorrow. Victor can fly home or walk or crawl, for all I care. I want to take action before anybody tries to talk some sense into me."

I know exactly what she means. Mama has never given up hope that I will reconcile with Jack. If she'd write all her bad advice down, she'd have two volumes of *How to Drive Your Daughter Crazy During Divorce.*

And speaking of Mama, my cell phone rings and her number pops up.

"Are you coming? We're already at the Rendezvous."

"So early?" It will be at least thirty minutes before we can get there, and then only with some of Fayrene's divine invention.

"There's a line a mile long. Charlie's put our name on the waiting list."

"Just save us a seat, Mama. And don't wait to order."

"Flitter. Who do you think I am? Mabel Moffett?" That's the biggest insult Mama can think of. Mabel has a reputation all over Mooreville for bad social graces. Most of it deserved, but still . . .

"Now, Mama," is all I say.

I do Mabel's hair. I'm not about to say anything ugly.

Chapter 16

Rendezvous, Mrs. Malaprop Reunited, and Seize the Day

Charlie Vergos' popular restaurant is just across the street. Though it's early, a line of hungry diners already snakes through the alley and down the stairs. We'll be here for hours.

Back in 1948, the Rendezvous was a modest eatery serving ham sandwiches. Then Charlie discovered a smokestack in his basement, fired up a barbecue pit, and put Memphis on the culinary map.

Mama and the gang are already downstairs, not far from the front of the line. She spots us and waves, purple sleeves billowing and bangles clanking every which way. She even calls "yoohoo!" which is Southernese for "over here."

We weave through the crowd and I see polecat hair. With none other than Victor Mabry. Jill sees them, too.

"What's your husband doing with Carolyn Mims?" Since we've already had a soul-baring session, this is not an impolite question. I pride myself on manners.

"Digging for dirt, and she's only too happy to dish it." Jill turns her back on them. "She's the prissy butt who tattled about me being in Grayson's room."

Victor notices his wife and barrels our way, but Uncle Charlie cuts him off. I'd give a thirty-dollar haircut to know what they're saying. From the thunderous look on Victor's face, it's not pretty.

Uncle Charlie rejoins our group and offers his arm to Jill. "Don't worry, my dear. He won't bother you this evening."

I'm glad, though it's not Victor's manners I'm thinking about; it's his connection to Carolyn Mims. Or more precisely, hers to him. Listen, if I had a sister-in-law who cut off ties to my family, I'd be in a killing mood. (If I were that type, which of course, I'm not.) Maybe it wasn't Grayson she consorted with to murder Babs. Maybe it was Victor.

The next chance I get, I'm asking Jill if Victor or Carolyn had any connection to Gloria Divine or Latoya LaBelle. Too, I'm going to find out if extreme stress makes Victor speak with a lisp. Why not? Stress is a factor in nearly every malady you can name.

My cell phone rings and Champ's number pops up. I hope nothing has happened to Hoyt and the cats. I open the phone and say hello, but the din is too loud.

"Champ, can you hear me? Hold on. I'm going outside."

It takes me a while to weave through the crowd. Even the stairs are packed with barbecue lovers trying to get down. Finally I reach the alley outside and the relative quiet of street traffic.

"Champ, I'm back. What's up?"

"I miss you."

If I had time to have a life, I might miss him, too. If Jack would sign divorce papers. If I were free to indulge in those emotions. If I could get my heart to agree with my head.

So many *ifs*. I wish I could replace them with a whole string of definites.

"Callie? Are you there?"

"I'm here. Bad connection." I cross my fingers behind my back so the little white lie won't count.

"Do you want me to hang up and call back?"

"No, it's better now. How are the animals?"

"They're all doing great, but that's not why I called. If you can stay an extra day at the Peabody, I'll come up when Charlie gets back and we can have a brief getaway."

That's a polite way of putting it. Jack would have put it another way.

All of a sudden I feel like crying. Don't ask me why.

"Callie? Say yes."

"Let me think about it. A lot's going on up here."

"Yeah. I heard about the Peabody murders. If Charlie weren't there, I would be."

"Look, you're sweet and thoughtful to call, and I really, really appreciate your taking care of my animals, but my family is waiting downstairs. We're having dinner at the Rendezvous."

"Enjoy. I'll call back later."

A conversation like that ought to make me feel

good. I don't even want to think about why it doesn't. Tucking the phone in my pocket, I push open the restaurant door. About that time, a jet flies over, low, coming in for a landing at Memphis Airport.

Jack. That's all I think. Just Jack.

I slide through the door and shut out the reminder.

When I get back Mama says, "Who was that?"

"Champ."

"Charlie says Jack's on the way."

Where Jack's concerned, Mama's completely transparent. Sometimes I find this annoying, but tonight it comforts me to know she cares enough to meddle.

"He gave me a good report on my animals."

"Well, if you ask me . . ."

"Ruby Nell." That's all Uncle Charlie says, and Mama drops the subject.

Our gang is seated at a long table next to a back wall. (What else? Uncle Charlie is here.) I slide in beside Lovie.

Jill is sitting beside Bobby Huckabee, whose face is blazing red. And if there's an inch of space between Fayrene and Jarvetis, I'd challenge a NASA engineer to find it.

The only one missing from our party is Elvis, who was miffed he couldn't come along. I explained that only guide dogs for the blind are allowed in restaurants, and I'll swear if he didn't nose open my tote bag and get my sunglasses. I guess he thinks all the seeing impaired wear them.

I just hope he's behaving himself.

Uncle Charlie signals the waiter, who comes

over to take our orders. Meanwhile, Mama and Fayrene are discussing the murders. I try to think of something else to talk about, anything besides murder and Jack Jones.

"Jarvetis, have you found your redbone hound?" Trey and Elvis are buddies, and don't tell me dogs don't have best friends.

"Not yet, but ole Trey won't go far. I know my redbone hound dogs."

Fayrene just twitches her eyebrows. Ordinarily, she'd make a remark such as, "I wish he knew his wife half as well," but apparently she's still under the spell of her hours-old reconciliation.

"You'll never guess who's coming home," she says. "Darlene!" Fayrene and Jarvetis' youngest daughter. Twice married. One child. A boy, I think.

And a manicurist. With Atlanta experience. I know the salon where she works and I know its reputation.

"For a visit or to stay?" Mama asks.

"She's staying this time. When she left Earl, she couldn't let her coattail touch her behind till she found somebody else, but she says she's through with marriage."

"Don't be too sure," Mama says. "She's a pretty little thing."

"She takes after me." Fayrene fans herself with her napkin. "I think she means it, though. She's had more problems with that sorry Wayne Grant than allegories in a swamp."

Lovie chokes on her water and I kick her under the table. Who knows? Maybe allegories are everywhere, and they're all out to get us.

"When will she be home?" I ask.

"Before Christmas. She's sure of that. Maybe before then."

The timing would be perfect. A new manicurist for Hair.Net just in time for the holidays. Lots of holiday promotions. Darlene might be the first step in turning my beauty shop into my south-of-Mooreville Riviera. If I can find the money.

Of course, I could be like Mama. Every time she writes a check, she says she's writing fiction. Which would be the truth if I hadn't set up a no-bounce account for her. If she knew, she'd put herself on the fiction bestseller list—and me on Skid Row with a tin cup.

I'm not going to think about any of that right now; I'm taking action, seizing the day.

"Fayrene, does she already have a job lined up?"

"Not yet, hon. But anybody with her talents is bound to have more offers than Jarvetis' hound has ticks."

"Trey does not have ticks," Jarvetis says, deadpan.

Judging by the twinkle in his eye, I'd say he knows Fayrene is just kidding. My guess is, he wants to keep her on her toes a while longer, make her work a bit harder at holding her man.

She pats his arm. "Of course, he doesn't, hon. You treat your redbone hound dog as well as you treat your family."

"Well, I wouldn't go that far. I don't sleep with him."

Everybody at the table cracks up. Jarvetis is a man of few words. Most of them spoken at Gas, Grits, and Guts. The few social gatherings he attends, he likes to sit quietly and watch Fayrene take the floor.

While I get Darlene's number, the waiter heads our way with two huge platters of ribs. The smell makes my mouth water.

"Dinner's on me," Jarvetis says, continuing his expansive mood. "Fayrene and I are celebrating. Everybody dig in."

"Everybody except you." Fayrene pats her husband's hand. "Remember, hon, your Geritol is high. I'd die if you had to have a heart castration."

Well, I guess she would!

Chapter 17

Long Island Ice Tea, Bad Decisions, and Unicorns

By the time we leave the Rendezvous, it's nearly ten o'clock. Our party walks out into a balmy night under one of those brilliant October skies you'd like to press between the pages of a memory album. Murder has no place in a night like this.

When Mama says, "Charlie, it's too pretty to go inside. Let's stroll to the river and watch the stars," I know she's thinking about Daddy.

I used to sneak out of bed and hunker down by the window to watch them on the front porch swing, holding hands while Daddy pointed out the constellations. His favorite was Orion the Hunter. One night I overheard him say, "Ruby Nell, when I die I'm going to become a star in Orion's belt. All you have to do is look up, and you'll see me."

I like to believe he did. As she and Uncle Charlie head toward the river, I like to imagine she'll look up and see Daddy shining over the water, watching over her still.

Fayrene and Jarvetis head to Mallards for a nightcap while Lovie, Bobby, Jill, and I make plans to enjoy a night on the town, but only in places that will allow dogs. Elvis needs a break.

They wait for me in the lobby while I catch the elevator. This time of evening it's packed, but I'm not about to start trying to figure out if one of the crowd is the Peabody murderer. I need a break, too.

Elvis is curled in the middle of Jill's bed, never mind that he has his own pillow.

"Get down from there, Elvis. You'll get dog hair on the covers."

He shows absolutely no remorse. When he clambers down, he takes so much time I could jog to Texas and back. Any longer, and you can add Mexico.

"We're going outside, boy. Sightseeing."

Don't tell me dogs don't understand when we talk to them as if they're people. By the time we return to the lobby, Elvis is prancing like the King he thinks he is.

As the five of us head into the neon lights, pulsating beats, and howling rhythms of Beale Street, Lovie punches me.

"Somebody's following us."

"A crowd's out tonight, Lovie. That's all."

"No. It's Victor."

I glance behind and, sure enough, Jill's husband darts behind two women I recognize as *Beige Housecoat* and *Foam Rollers*. What are they doing out at this time of night? They look so tired they ought to be bundled in afghans in front of the TV.

I put my finger over my lips so Lovie won't blurt out the name of our stalker. No need to ruin Jill's evening. Besides, we have Elvis and Bobby Huckabee. What can go wrong?

Our first destination is Handy Park on the corner of Beale and Third. I resist the urge to look over my shoulder to see if Victor is still following. What can he do in this crowd?

Unless he's the killer, of course, who has a record of picking off his victims in crowds. I don't see him now, but as we enter the park, Bobby says, "There's danger all around."

I get the shivers and Jill jerks like she's been shot.

"What? What did you say?"

"He said there's dancing all around," I tell Jill. Which is not a complete lie.

Music pours from every club, the kind of blues that won't let your feet stand still. Overcome by the rhythm, some couples are swaying in the streets.

Or maybe they're just overcome with Long Island Ice Tea. Handy Park is across the street from the Rum Boogie Café, and that potent five-liquor drink is their specialty.

Bobby shakes his head like a man coming out of a trance. "We're standing on the very street where Martin Luther King Jr. made his last march. The vibes are so powerful here I feel like my bones are shaking in two."

Jill's getting spooked. Lovie sees this, too, and takes her arm.

"What we need is a drink." She waves to Bobby and me. "You two go on and let Elvis do his business. I'm taking Jill to Rum Boogie."

They head across the street to the old brick building with its primitive mural on the outside wall. "Barrelhouse, Boogie and the Blues" it proclaims, and a happy, painted couple gyrates to the rhythms rocking through the door. After Jill and Lovie leave, I tell Bobby to be careful of his predictions around Jill.

"She's going through a rough time right now, and we're trying to help her forget her problems."

"I'm sorry, Callie. Really. I never do think." He shakes his head and looks so despairing that I pat his arm.

"That's okay, Bobby."

"I guess you've wondered why a man of my looks and position doesn't have a girl."

I'm glad Lovie's not here. I'd have to punch her black and blue to hold her mirth. Poor Bobby. I'm glad his mirror lies.

"Well," I say, and then I can't think of anything else.

"It's my psychic eye. It scares everybody off. I guess I'm just hopeless."

"Absolutely not, Bobby. The right woman hasn't come along, that's all. Who knows? You might meet her tomorrow."

"I hope she likes Vanna White."

"I hope so, too, Bobby." What else is there to say?

We join a large group of tourists and music lovers in the park to pay homage to W.C. Handy. Not to be outshone by the Father of the Blues or any of the luminaries whose influence still reigns on Beale—B.B. King, Al Green, Howlin' Wolf, Carl Perkins, Isaac Hayes—Elvis starts marking bushes and trying to give autographs. (I swear, that's what it looks like.) He keeps prancing up to strangers, shaking his head so his mismatched ears flop, and extending his paw.

"He's a ham," Bobby says.

"He thinks he's the King of Rock 'n' Roll."

"Is he?"

"I don't know. He could be."

I pride myself on an open mind, even regarding Bobby's psychic eye. Everybody in Mooreville knows it. That's one of the reasons my beauty shop is so popular. My customers know they can tell me any crazy notion that pops into their heads and I'll give it the same serious consideration Thomas Jefferson put into penning the Declaration of Independence.

After Elvis finishes his business, we head back across the street to join Lovie and Jill. They've found a sidewalk table and, thank goodness, it's backed up to an outside wall. I'll see everybody who approaches, including Victor. Though what would I do if he did? Hit him over the head with my designer shoes?

"What took you so long? We got a head start." Lovie indicates two glasses on the table, already empty.

Bobby and I each order a Long Island Ice Tea, then I sit back to enjoy some down and dirty Delta blues spilling onto the sidewalk. A gravel-voiced singer is inside belting out "3 O'Clock in the Morning Blues"—which just about says it all.

Don't get me started on Jack.

When my drink comes, I take a sip and nearly fall out of my chair. There's enough tequila and vodka and rum and I don't know what else in this concoction to fell a horse. Another sip and my lips go numb.

Listen, Long Island Ice Tea just might be the best idea Lovie has had the entire trip. One more sip and I'll be imagining myself as Lady Godiva reincarnated. Who knows? Somebody around here is bound to have a horse. Everything else would fade in comparison to riding sidesaddle down the street naked.

Except maybe Jack.

I reach for my drink. And this time I take a slug.

Lovie orders another round of drinks, then out of the blue, she says, "Jill and I have decided to get tattoos."

"Doggone." I slap my thigh. "Why not?"

When we finally leave, it takes us a while (Southernese for anything from ten minutes to ten days) to walk two blocks to the parlor. All those conniving cracks in the sidewalk, not to mention the prankster light poles that keep getting in the way.

Two years later (to say the least) we walk into a little shop that smells like sandalwood and sage. Everything's a blur after that. All I remember is having to take a cab back to the Peabody.

I'm happy to wake up at a decent hour, which means Elvis didn't drag me out for a pre-dawn pee and nobody murdered Mama. Or Jill. Or Lovie. Or me.

Or did they? I've either died and gone the wrong way or I have a hangover the size of Montana.

Ordinarily, I'd turn on the TV and listen to the news. Lovie's such a sound sleeper, she could sleep through a level-five hurricane.

But I don't want my head to explode. Plus Jill's curled into a little snoozing ball on the other bed, and I don't want to risk disturbing her. She's going to need every ounce of energy to keep her plan intact after she drives back to Paris and two dozen Tennessee relatives start telling her what to do.

Maybe some fresh air will help. I wince when I slide into sweats. What in the world is going on?

Tiptoeing into the bathroom, I back up to the full length mirror and take a peek. Holy cow! A unicorn's staring back at me. From a place where the sun doesn't shine.

A *unicorn*, of all things. My pet name for Jack. Our secret love code. I think I will dig a little hole behind the Peabody, crawl in, and pull the dirt over my head.

Or maybe I'll just go for a run.

I put on my Air Nikes, then grab Elvis' leash and we head for the park.

Last night as we left the Rendezvous, Uncle Charlie took me aside and said Jack will be in Memphis today. At 2 P.M. if his plane is on time and *who knows when* if it's not.

In spite of knowing what I know about The Company, I don't have any idea what I'm going to say to him. Which is awful. You'd think by this time, I could either say, "Jack, sign the papers, it's over" or, "Jack, I've made a foolish mistake, come home."

Right now, though, all I'm thinking is, Lord, please don't let him find my unicorn.

When I'm stressed out, a hard run helps.

Ignoring the occasional stab in my hip, I unsnap Elvis' leash and the two of us run until I'm covered with sweat and his tongue is hanging out. He sinks onto the grass; I sink onto a bench.

Rule number two for beating the blues: take action. As long as you don't get a tattoo.

If you're surrounded by events beyond your control, it makes you feel infinitely better to do something you can control. Unless it's a tattoo.

Before I can change my mind, I whip out my cell phone and dial. I get right to the point.

"Champ? This is really a bad time for us to have a weekend getaway. Can I take a rain check?"

"Absolutely. I don't want to rush you, Callie. Take your time. I'm not going anywhere."

When I hang up, I'm breathing easier. The second call I make is to Atlanta.

"Darlene, this is Callie Valentine Jones." No need to elaborate. She knows who I am and what I do. For once, I'm grateful for Fayrene's habit of telling everything she knows.

"If you don't already have employment plans, I'd like to hire you as manicurist at Hair.Net."

Darlene asks all the right questions and apparently I give all the right answers because she says yes. I silently shout *yes*, *yes* while she tells me more about herself.

Afterward, I head back to the hotel to share the good news with Lovie. The TV's on, and she's on the phone with Rocky, sounding like a call girl on a nine hundred number. Jill is nowhere in sight. In no mood to listen to love talk, even if Lovie is my best friend, I go into the bathroom, shut the door, and take a shower, being careful to keep the soap off my unicorn.

Lovie bursts in while I'm in mid-soap. Nobody in this family knocks. When I get back to Mooreville, I'm going to conduct a remedial manners class. Valentines, only.

"I had Rocky going this time."

"I don't want to hear about Rocky's libido." I stick my head out of the shower and glare at her. "Why did you let me get a tattoo?"

"I didn't *let* you. You insisted."

"Yeah, but you knew I was in no condition to be sensible."

"Live, that's what I say."

"Yes, but *this*?"

"Turn around. Let me see it."

I oblige and she's quiet for so long I think she's passed out. Finally she says, "He's even cuter sober than he was drunk."

"I don't think he was drunk, Lovie. That was you and me."

"Speak for yourself." She starts prissing out, and I yell after her.

"Wait a minute. What did *you* get?"

Lovie lifts the hem of her nightshirt and wags her backside at me. Holy cow. Emblazoned across both hips in bold red letters are the words *national treasure*.

She turns around, grinning. "Well?"

"You have finally rendered me speechless."

"Good. Let's hope I have that same effect on Rocky."

Lovie prances out and I finish my shower. It's already midmorning and we have dirt to dig and secrets to uncover.

Chapter 18

Masked Madness, Toilet Trickery, and Peeping Tom

When I reenter the bedroom, Lovie's propped on her pillows eating a bag of corn curls and watching TV.

"I forgot to ask. Where's Jill?"

"Gone home. She wanted to get an early start. Said to tell you thank you and she'd stay in touch."

"What about Victor?"

A reporter on Channel Five interrupts a game show rerun—as well as Lovie and me—with a late-breaking bulletin on the Peabody killer.

"The police say they are still questioning witnesses but, so far, no suspects have been taken into custody."

The reporter shoves the microphone at Chief of Police Miller Stewart. "My sources say the MPD will be out in force at today's dance competition finale at the Peabody. Do you expect to make an arrest?"

"Let me assure you, the Memphis Police Department will catch this killer. As for the particulars, no comment."

I grab a pair of sequined leather Manolo Blahnik heels. If there's a chase, let the MPD do it.

"We never heard a peep from Victor," Lovie says.

"That can't be good. I wonder what he's up to?"

"We don't have time to discuss it. The competition finale starts in five minutes. They're serving brunch, and I'm starving."

Lovie tosses the empty snack bag into the garbage, then jerks on a flimsy costume hardly big enough for a midget.

"If you expect me to zip that, you're out of your mind."

Her costume is gaping two inches. Zipping it will take a miracle on the order of the parting of the Red Sea.

"You're just jealous about my national treasure."

"Don't make me laugh, Lovie. I'm mad at you." I grab her zipper and try to haul it upward.

"Pull, Callie."

"It's stuck. Why don't you wear something else?" Sans dance costume makes sense to me. She's decided not to do the jitterbug competition so she wouldn't be competing against Uncle Charlie.

She says a word that will get her barred from public places, sucks in enough air to propel a clipper ship across the Pacific, and gets the zipper closed. It'll take an act of Congress to get it open again. But I'm not going to worry about that, yet.

For once, Elvis is satisfied to be left alone. I guess he's still tuckered out from his morning run. Not to mention his late night prowl on Beale Street.

We hurry downstairs, making plans as we go.

With all the dancers in one room, it's the perfect time to ask questions, then break and enter. I'm not keen on the idea, but we still don't know anything about the third victim. And we certainly need to know what Thomas Whitenton has been up to, besides *no good* with Mama.

The finale is in the Peabody's glorious Continental Ballroom. Enormous crystal chandeliers and Venetian-style frescoes make me feel as if I've stepped back into a more genteel time when women embraced femininity and men practiced courtliness. I'm glad I opted for sequined shoes.

Mama and Uncle Charlie are not here yet, but Fayrene and Jarvetis meet us at the door. Both are holding Elvis masks.

"They're giving them to everybody." Fayrene puts hers on. "Tonight is tribute night to the King. Be sure to get yours."

I think I'll get one for Elvis, just for kicks.

"Can you believe Grayson is here?" She nods toward the baby grand piano where he's standing with his sister and trying to balance two loaded plates from the buffet. "You'd think he'd be prostate with grief."

I have a hard time keeping my face straight and Lovie covers her giggle with a cough.

"Maybe he was hungry," she says. "I certainly am."

Lovie barrels toward the buffet tables, but I lag behind and try to think of something nice to say.

"Break a leg in the jitterbug competition."

"Lord, I hope not," Jarvetis says, and Fayrene pats his hand. "Hon, it's theater jargon for good luck."

By the time I catch up with Lovie, she's halfway through a plate of cheese grits with shrimp.

"Needs less salt and more cheese."

The only thing she's picky about is food. She looks on it as a source of hedonistic pleasure while I view it as sustenance. Putting fresh fruit on my plate, I glance around the room. There's a cop in every corner, but still no sign of Mama and Uncle Charlie. I'm wondering whether I need to call one of them when Victor strolls into the ballroom.

"Lovie, look." I nod toward the door. "You take Grayson and Carolyn, I'll take Victor. Meet you in the ladies' room in fifteen minutes."

By the time I get across the dance floor, Victor's wearing his Elvis mask. And he's none too happy to see me.

"You!" Victor Mabry has the charm of a squash. No wonder Jill is leaving him.

He turns to leave, but I say, "Wait, I want to talk to you."

"Meddling again, Ms. Jones?" I guess my surprise shows, and Victor sneers at me. "I make it a point to find out who my enemies are."

"I'm not your enemy, Victor. I just rescued your wife."

"If you don't butt out of my business, you're the one who's going to need rescuing." He stalks off, but I've found out two things I wanted to know: under stress, Victor Mabry does not speak with a lisp, and he's capable of great anger. But is it enough to have killed the woman he loved and lost? And what motive could he possibly have had for killing the other two?

Grabbing a mask for my dog, I head toward the

ladies' room. The buffet tables are being cleared, and out of the corner of my eye, I see Lovie refilling her plate. She catches up with me in the hall.

"Standing up ruins my digestion." She plops into a Queen Anne loveseat while I tell her what I found out. It's not nearly as much as she did, though.

"Grayson was extremely jealous of Victor and any other man who looked at his wife."

"What about the lisp, Lovie?"

"Not a sign with Grayson, but Carolyn has one. It's slight, but it's there. And she fairly well hated her sister-in-law."

"Did you smell anything? Old Spice aftershave? A perfume that Mama might have mistaken for that?"

"Yes. But there were so many people standing around I couldn't tell where it was coming from."

I have a feeling we're getting close. Lovie's reaching for a chocolate covered strawberry when an unholy scream rips the air. We race toward the sound while cops pour out of the ballroom and thunder right behind us toward the restrooms.

A masked man bolts from the ladies' room. Two cops give chase while two more sprint past us and into the restroom.

Lovie and I burst through the doors and Jarvetis roars in right behind us.

The screams are coming from none other than Fayrene, who is attached to the toilet door by her green silk scarves. Red faced and bulgy eyed, she looks as if she's being strangled Isadora Duncan style.

"It's the killer," she screeches.

"Now, hon." Jarvetis grabs her scarves and starts untangling. "You just got your scarves caught and you panicked, that's all."

Apparently he didn't see the man scuttling from the restroom. While the cops take Fayrene's statement, Lovie and I hurry back into the hallway to see what we can find out about the masked mystery man.

Nothing, it looks like. The hallway is empty.

Lovie leans against the wall. "If I run another step I'm going to need oxygen."

"I wanted to see who that masked man was."

"It wasn't Thomas. He couldn't have run that fast with a banged-up leg."

"I distinctly saw him limping."

"You just want it to be him, Callie. What in the world would be his motive? The only thing we know for sure is that all the killings took place near the ducks."

"Maybe the ducks did it." She gives me this look. Usually she's the one making smart-mouth remarks. "Besides, you're forgetting the attempts on Fayrene and Mama."

"Aunt Ruby Nell's a drama queen and Fayrene's got the biggest imagination in Mooreville."

"How does that explain Mama clubbing Thomas with the baseball bat?"

"Maybe there are two killers."

"I hadn't thought of that. It would explain why we've found no connection between Babs' murder and the other two."

"We're not through yet. Come on." Lovie grabs my arm and starts hustling me toward the ballroom. Apparently there's nothing like playing detective to give Lovie a second wind.

We're in sight of the ballroom when I spot cops down a side hall. Collaring a man wearing an Elvis mask.

"Lovie, quick. This way."

If that masked Elvis is Mama's constant companion, I want to be the first to know.

Elvis' Opinion #8 on Entrepreneurship, Escape, and Felonious Cats

Do you think I'd be stuck in this room if I didn't want to be? Naturally I pretended to be sulking about not going to the dance finale. I didn't want Callie to get suspicious.

Listen, I have big plans that go way beyond who killed the three dancers. This is my town. I plan to figure a way to escape while Callie and Lovie are gone.

My public is waiting. I got a taste of them last night at the park named for that other musician whose fame does not even approach my iconic status.

Now I'm all fired up to sashay down the street in my pink bowtie and cut another record at Sun Studios. Maybe sign a few paw prints on the way. Then I want to mosey back up to Beale Street and sit in on a gut-bucket blues jam session, recapture the good old days, bask in the accolades, feel my sap running high.

Maybe I'll even pay a visit to the gift shop, see if I can scare up a Lansky, then see about having a bell-bottom jumpsuit made. Of course, it would feature four legs, but who cares. If anybody can make four legs all the rage, it's me.

I prance over to the door, cock my mismatched ears, and listen for sounds of the maid. The first little sign of activity in the hallway and I plan to set up such a howl, somebody will come running and open the door.

That'll be all she wrote. I'll be outta here, baby. Adios. Sayonara. Toot, toot, tootsie, good-bye.

Naturally, I'll be back. I'd never permanently run away. Callie needs me. Especially now that she's hired a new woman for Hair.Net.

I'm not saying a manicurist is a bad thing. In fact, it's a smart entrepreneurial move. Even Darlene is not a bad choice. The only thing wrong with her is the entourage that comes along with her.

Don't think I didn't hear both ends of the phone conversation at the river. I can live with a little boy in the beauty shop. In fact, I plan to teach him a few tricks. How to dig a hole to China. How to bury treasure all over the backyard. I might even teach him how to spit.

What I can't deal with is Darlene's cat. *Mal*, she calls him. What kind of name is that? It's too short. Lacking class. Without character. It's bound to stand for something else. Probably Malicious. Malevolent. Malcontent. Maladjusted. Maladroit.

Heck, for all I know, it stands for Malarkey. Whatever it stands for, it can't be good.

Hair.Net's not big enough for me and a cat. One of us will have to go. And I can guarantee you, it won't be me.

Guess what's right across the street from Gas, Grits, and Guts in beautiful downtown Mooreville? A fireworks place.

Have you ever seen what a few firecrackers tied to a cat's tail will do? Let me put it this way: Mal will be lucky if he stops running before he gets to the Alabama state line.

Hold your horses. Is that the sound of little rubber wheels in the hallway? I hunker down with my ears perked up. It looks like I'm going to get my chance to blow this joint.

Chapter 19

Misdemeanors, Felonies, and Jitterbug

I don't know why I said, "Quick." If I'd known I'd be running all over the place, I would never have worn four-inch heels.

By the time Lovie and I halt our momentum enough to reverse direction and turn the corner, the cops are leading the suspect off.

"Wait!" I yell.

The prime suspect turns his head, sans mask. Alas, the man in cuffs is not Thomas; it's Victor.

I'm sorry to say I'm disappointed, which means I have a lot of work to do on myself in the milk-of-human-kindness department. It looks like I'll stoop to all kinds of vengeful thinking to get what I want—Mr. Whitenton out of Mama's life.

One of the cops separates himself from the group and heads our way. Fortunately, it's a grandfatherly looking gray-haired man and not the baby cop who already has me on his pain-in-the-neck list.

Lovie says a word that could get us both arrested

while I try to act as if I'm not going all over the Peabody interfering in police business.

"Do you ladies have something to tell me?"

"Is that the Peabody killer?" I ask.

"Names?" The cop whips out his notebook and Lovie punches me. Hard.

"She's just scared, that's all. So many dancers dying." Lovie fakes a convincing shiver that sets every sequin on her costume aquiver. The cop smiles. A good sign. "We were headed to the bathroom."

Now she's prancing up and down like she can barely hold her water. Sometimes I think Lovie's in the wrong profession. I can see her on Broadway or filling the silver screen in a B-grade movie. Shoot, with Lovie, it could even be A-list. After all, she is a national treasure.

"The ladies' room's that way." He nods his head in the direction of the restrooms, starts to leave, then turns back. "Didn't I see you in the restroom earlier?"

"Yes, but we were just there to touch up our lipstick." Lovie was always quick on her feet, but I don't think she has fooled the man in uniform.

"You ladies stay out of trouble." He pockets his notebook and rejoins the police who are escorting Victor out the door.

"They'll probably book Victor for felony," Lovie says.

"I don't know if being a peeping Tom is a felony."

There's a lot I don't know. And not just about this case. For instance, I don't know what I'll do when Jack arrives.

My phone rings, rattling the last nerve I have left. It's Mama.

"Where are you? The jitterbug competition's about to start and Bobby's looking for Lovie."

"She's not going to compete against Uncle Charlie."

"Flitter. Fayrene and Jarvetis are competing against us."

"She's dancing? After what happened in the ladies' room?"

"It'll take more than somebody hiding behind an Elvis mask to stop Fayrene. Besides, Jarvetis hasn't danced since 1989. She's not about to let this chance get away. Hurry."

I pocket my cell phone. "We have our marching orders." I repeat Mama's conversation to Lovie.

"I wanted to see Daddy dance anyway."

"So do I. Besides, it will give us a chance to see who's there and who's not. I still want to get into Thomas' room."

"So do I."

"Shoot, Lovie. I thought you believed the cops had caught the killer."

"I just want another chance to check out the re-action to my maid's outfit. You never know. It could come in handy down in Mexico."

If anybody can mix archeology and kinkiness, it's Lovie. As we head toward the Continental Ballroom, I send a silent prayer into the universe that Lovie's trip to visit Rocky will be everything she wants it to be.

The buffet tables have been cleared, the jitterbug competition is already in full swing, and Bobby Huckabee meets us at the door.

"Ruby Nell said to watch for you."

I spot Mama and Uncle Charlie doing a tight,

pitch-perfect jitterbug near the center of the dance floor. Fayrene and Jarvetis are nearby. Gyrating every which way, they almost knock over the barrier separating the judges' stand from the dance floor. They correct their direction so fast they barely miss knocking over a geriatric couple shimmying at snail speed. (What they lack in skill, they make up for in enthusiasm.)

"Looks like Fayrene and Jarvetis are giving Daddy and Aunt Ruby Nell a run for their money."

"I wouldn't go so far as to say that, Lovie."

Naturally, I'm prejudiced, but I think Mama and Uncle Charlie are surefire winners. They look like they've been dancing together for years. And who knows? Maybe they have. They're pros at keeping secrets.

Who would have believed my uncle had been leading a double life? Mama, too. I didn't find out till the Bubbles Caper that she smokes. She could also have been a deep cover agent in The Company, and I'd never know.

"I've got seats saved," Bobby says.

He barrels ahead, reeking hair gel and moving so fast even Lovie has a hard time keeping up. I can see why he doesn't have a girlfriend. He has the style and social grace of a toad. As soon as we get back to Mooreville, I'm going to offer him a few pointers. In a kind way, of course. Nobody wants to think of himself as lacking charm.

As we trail along in his wake, I scan the crowd for Thomas Whitenton. Lovie's doing the same thing. People are milling about, which makes it hard to find him. To complicate matters, many of them are already wearing Elvis masks in spite of the fact that the competition will last the rest of the day and the Elvis tribute dance won't start till evening.

"I guess I could go around snatching off masks." Lovie would do it, too, if she thought it would help her family.

"We have all day, Lovie. Be patient."

Bobby is waiting for us in the third row. I sit next to him, trying to keep my ulterior motives from showing. You never know. If Bobby really does have an all-seeing blue eye, he'd sniff out my intent to go snooping in the maid's uniform.

"Have you seen Thomas?"

Bobby doesn't react like a suspicious man, which casts serious doubts on his psychic abilities.

"He's here," Bobby says.

"Where?"

Bobby glances around the ballroom, perplexed. "Well. He was here a minute ago."

"Oh, great." Lovie rolls her eyes.

"Yeah. How about that?" Bobby says. "And him with a bandaged leg."

Strike two for the psychic eye. Lovie's irony whizzes right over Bobby. But it's not him I'm worried about: it's unmasking Thomas Whitenton before he kills my mother.

The jitterbug competition is winding down, and time is running out. Lovie and I need to leave before the dance is over. If we don't, we'll have a hard time escaping Mama and Uncle Charlie. She's already miffed about being left out of *all the fun* and he's already warned me to lie low and let Jack handle things.

That's the last thing I need. Every time I let Jack handle my things, I end up between the sheets in my house or backed up against the rinse sinks at Hair.Net.

If Lovie and I don't get into Thomas Whitenton's room before my almost-ex gets in from China, we might as well forget it. Skirting around the senior Valentines is one thing; skirting around Jack Jones is a whole 'nother ball game.

Suddenly Lovie elbows me and nods toward the door. Thomas has appeared with two cups of punch, probably one for him, one for Mama. He's certainly not bringing Uncle Charlie something cool to drink, especially after the twin humiliations of being flogged and being beat out of a chance to show his stuff on the dance floor with Ruby Nell Valentine.

Lovie nudges me again. Hard. I'm going to get her for this.

"Oh my goodness! I almost forgot." I glance at my watch, feigning panic. "Lovie, if we don't hurry, we'll miss our spa appointment."

As we stand up to leave, Bobby says, "If you'll leave your key, I'll check on Elvis after the competition." He winks at me. "While you snoop."

We stop dead in our tracks. When we turn around to face Bobby again, Lovie's mouth is hanging open. I guess mine is, too, because it takes me a while to say anything.

"How did you know?"

"Psychic eye." He winks again.

"What's it telling you about the Peabody killer?"

"There's danger from a dark-eyed stranger."

Holy cow! I should have known better than to believe in his psychic eye.

"It's not what you're thinking," he says. "The dark-eyed stranger of this vision is somebody you know, somebody who could rain hellfire and brimstone on the head of the killer."

That would be only one person. Jack Jones.

Fishing in my purse, I find my room key and hand it to Bobby.

"Thanks for looking after Elvis. I'll call you after we've finished our . . ." What's the nice way to put what we're planning to do?

"Snooping," Lovie says, winking at him, then we hightail it out of the ballroom.

We race as fast as we dare without calling attention to ourselves. We're making good progress till Lovie suddenly vanishes. One minute she's beside me, the next she's gone.

"What on earth?"

"Shhh." Her hiss is coming from behind a potted palm. She reaches out and snatches me behind the scraggly tree so fast I nearly break the heel of my Manolo Blahniks. "Somebody's after us."

"What do you mean, *after us*?"

"I distinctly heard somebody behind me whisper, 'Die, hoothie mama.' "

"Hoothie?"

"*Hoochie*, Callie. Has your mind taken a leave of absence?"

I don't generally take exception to Lovie's remarks because I know she has my best interests at heart. But I'm full of frazzled nerves and plane-from-China anxiety, and I'm lucky to remember my own name. I'm fixing to take exception.

"I wouldn't cast aspersions on my mind if I'd picked the scrawniest palm in the entire room to hide behind. Good grief, Lovie. It's the width of a swizzle stick."

In her sequined dress, Lovie is the approximate size of Arkansas. She's shining through the branches like sunrise over the Pacific. But I stop short of telling her all that. I pride myself on being nice to everybody, even when I'm mad.

Lovie says that's one of my major faults. Actually what she always tells me is, "Get some backbone, show some spunk." Maybe she's right. Maybe after all this is over, I'll work on the assertive side of my personality.

"Sarcasm doesn't become you, Callie."

"You use it all the time."

"It suits me." She cranes her neck around the palm. "All clear. Let's hustle."

When we get to the fourth floor, Elvis is nowhere to be seen. He doesn't even come when I call, but that's not unusual. Elvis has a take it or leave it attitude about obedience. Mostly, he leaves it.

When that happens I do what every smart dog owner does, I resort to bribery. This time it's a Milk-Bone treat.

"Elvis, want a cookie?"

Lovie snorts. "If you want a male to come, give him something worth coming over." She digs into her stash for a doughnut. "Doughnut, Elvis. Get your fat butt out here."

He waddles out, snatches the doughnut, then retreats back into the closet without even coming by to lick my ankles. I swear, when I get back to Mooreville, I'm putting him in obedience school.

Right now, though, I have to change. And fast.

Lovie and I start shucking clothes. Correction. I shuck, she's stuck. I grab her zipper and tug while she says words that ought to make the Guinness Book of Bad Language.

"Suck in, Lovie."

"I'm sucking. They're not making size twelve as big as they used to."

Holy cow! No wonder I'm going to have to rip seams and break the zipper. If she's a twelve, I'm Donald Trump.

Two ripped seams and a broken fingernail later, Lovie and her dress part company. We get in maid disguise, then race toward the elevators, hightailing it from a room that looks like somebody slaughtered a sequined goose.

For once the gods of wacky women are with us. The only person on the elevator is a petite blue-haired woman wearing a hearing aid and glasses with Coke-bottle lenses. Squinting up at Lovie, she says, "Young woman, that's a nice hat you're wearing."

"Wig's on backward," I whisper.

Lovie flips it back around, fluffs it up, and winks at the woman. "I like the feathers in front."

"I must say, it does look better."

The elevator inches upward, and though it stops at every floor, nobody else gets on. The bantam-size, nearsighted woman probably pushed every button.

She gets off on the tenth and totters down the hall. If she goes any slower, she won't make it to her room till Thanksgiving. There's no way we can break and enter while she's in sight.

"I could yell fire," Lovie says.

The mood I'm in, I'm about ready to let her. Which just goes to show the levels you'll sink to when murder enters the picture.

The poor little woman finally makes it to her room. I'm about to say *the coast is clear* when I spot the back of the most delicious man God ever put in the path of a Valentine woman.

"Quick, Lovie. Hide. The stairs."

Thank goodness she doesn't ask questions till we're inside the stairwell.

"Is it the cops?"

"Worse. Jack."

"You're sure?"

"Even if my eyes deceive me, my libido never does."

Let me come within yelling distance of Jack Jones and you can hear my motor revving all the way to the Mississippi River.

Lovie says a word that could bring down the roof. "At the rate we're going, we'll never get into Thomas' room."

My sentiments exactly. But I don't tell Lovie that. I pride myself on acting optimistic, even when I'm feeling exactly the opposite.

Which is why I'm going to face Jack head-on this time. Look him in the face and say: I want a life. I want a child. I want a divorce.

Of course, I have to get out of the stairwell first.

"Let's go, Lovie."

"Make up your mind. Are we coming or going?"

"Cute, Lovie." I barrel out and she's right behind me.

"Just when I'm getting to like this place."

In the hall, I pull down my short skirt and stick out my chin, geared for battle.

Alas, the enemy has left the corridor.

Chapter 20

X-rated Capers, Balconies, and Busted

Fortunately, nobody else is in the corridor, either. We head toward Thomas' room and it takes Lovie less than five seconds to get us in.

"If you ever decide to give up catering, you could make it picking locks."

"What's got you in such a piss and vinegar mood?"

"I've made up my mind. I'm standing firm with Jack this time. No more pussyfooting around."

"Great."

Lovie is a woman of action, let the consequences fall where they may. She would have already decided between Jack and Champ. Since I've been in pre-divorce limbo, I've lost count of the number of times she's said to me, "Quit dilly-dallying. You never know how something's going to turn out till you try it."

Now she's standing with her hands on her hips surveying Thomas' room. He brought enough stuff from Mississippi to hold a small garage sale on the Peabody's tenth floor.

"There's no telling what we'll find buried in all this junk," she says.

"Let's hope it's not another body."

"Let's ransack this place and find out. I'll start with the bathroom."

This could take a while. Now that I'm this close, I'm not even sure I want to find evidence that Thomas is the killer. What kind of daughter am I, hoping my mother's dance partner is a murderer? When I get home I'm lighting white candles and burning sacred white sage.

I glance around the room, trying to decide where to start. Obviously Thomas likes to take his treasures with him. In addition to three suitcases, he has shoeboxes stacked three deep on the closet floor. The desk in the corner has so many stacks of fat manila envelopes, you can hardly see the lamp.

"Find anything in the bathroom, Lovie?"

"Relief."

The toilet flushes and she comes out tugging at her uniform.

"What'd you see in there, Lovie?"

"Thomas pees on the toilet rim."

"Get serious. Anything of interest?"

"He uses frownies."

"Oh, good grief, Lovie. You take the desk, I'll take the closet."

If Lovie gets on her knees, it might be Christmas before I get her back up. Hiking my tight skirt up past decency, I sit cross-legged on the closet floor and open the first of eighteen boxes. Inside are Florsheims. Black patent. Although the soles show lots of wear, on the top you can hardly tell these shoes from brand new.

The next two boxes also hold Florsheims polished to a high shine. I wish I'd known this about Thomas earlier. A man who loves shoes can't be all bad.

I'm reaching for the fourth box when Lovie says, "Callie, you'd better have a look."

I unfold my long legs, stretch to get the kinks out, then join Lovie at the desk. There's a stack of empty envelopes at her elbow and an array of photographs fanned across the desktop. Even when they are upside down I can see that most of them feature Mama. Who can miss her bright yellow caftan and Queen of England crown jewels?

Going around the desk, I lean over Lovie's shoulder. There's Mama getting out of her red convertible in front of her monument company, Mama on the farm standing at the lake, Mama on her front porch sipping iced tea. I hope. With Mama you never can tell.

"These look candid."

"Yeah. I wonder if Thomas took them without Aunt Ruby Nell knowing."

A chilling thought. Even more chilling is the photograph Lovie points out. The beautiful woman playing with her dog in front of a giant magnolia tree is none other than Babs Mabry Mims.

I pick the photograph up to study it more closely. Babs is in severe need of a good haircut.

"Of course," Lovie says, "we've already established that he knows Babs."

"Yeah, but this one is just like the ones of Mama. Unposed."

"How do you know?"

"No woman with any pride is going to let somebody take her picture when her hair looks that bad."

Lovie takes the picture from me and lines it up beside the ones of Mama. "Look at this, Cal. They're all made from a distance."

"What does that prove besides Thomas doesn't know how to use a telephoto lens?"

"Maybe he wasn't aiming for art. Maybe he was a murderer stalking his prey with a camera."

Now I'm wishing I hadn't ducked into the stairwell when I saw Jack. I'm wishing I'd asked him to break and enter with us and help us get to the bottom of all this before the next victim turns out to be somebody I can't live without. Mama. Lovie. Uncle Charlie.

Except for one big thing. "Lovie, do you realize not a single one of the murder victims has been a man?"

"You're right." Suddenly Lovie says a word that peels paint. "Remember what the attacker said to Aunt Ruby Nell? And me? The killer's looking for 'hoochie mamas.' "

"Keep digging, Lovie. We're going to search every inch of this room."

I head back to the closet to see if I can find something besides Florsheims. In the next box, I do, but it's only a pair of Air Nikes that could use a good spritz of deodorant foot powder.

I'm about to despair, but on the last box I hit pay dirt.

"Holy cow! Lovie, come quick."

In my hot little hand is a three-volume set of

DVDs: "The fully restored 'XXX Diaries.'" Starring none other than Gloria Divine and Latoya La-Belle.

"Bingo," Lovie says. "Victims two and three."

Which brings another chilling thought: if he really is the killer, we could be next.

"Maybe we ought to call the police, Lovie. Or at least Uncle Charlie."

"Forget it. Playing safe is no fun."

She snatches the DVD set from me and shoves the first disc into the player on top of Thomas' TV.

"What are you doing?"

"I'm fixing to view the evidence."

"We're not the cops, Lovie."

"First come, first served."

"We could get in big trouble, here, Lovie."

"Are you going to sit in the closet all day and argue?"

Lovie has made herself at home on Thomas' bed, and is now leaning against the headboard on both pillows, her feet crossed at the ankles. This is what she does when we watch movies at home. She's settled in for the duration. All she needs is buttered popcorn.

I feel like Custer staging his last stand.

"We can't stay here, Lovie. Thomas is liable to come back."

"Put the night latch on. I'm not leaving till I see this."

"The night latch is already on. I did that after we broke in. I also hung up the DO NOT DISTURB sign."

"Well, what are you waiting for? Get your skinny butt over here before you miss the show."

I do what she says, but I refuse to sit on the bed. Instead, I drag the desk chair closer and plop down.

The names of the dubious "stars" flash across the screen and the camera pans a set that looks like something out of *Arabian Nights*. Amid the crash of cymbals and the twanging of exotic stringed instruments, two women slither onto the set. Gloria Divine and Latoya LaBelle—younger, more voluptuous versions of the woman found floating in the Peabody fountain in a Technicolor dress and the woman strangled with her own scarf at the duck parade.

I wouldn't call what they're doing *a show*. To put a polite spin on it, we've uncovered Thomas' stash of exotic entertainment.

"Where'd they learn to dance like that?" Lovie says.

"Not in Sunday school. I wouldn't even call it dancing."

"What would you call it?"

"Foreplay."

"Just because Jack's in the hotel . . ."

"Jack has nothing to do with it. Besides, he's out of the picture."

"Good. You'll feel better once you make a complete break."

Will I? I don't think I have Lovie's capacity to live my life forward, make instant decisions, keep what I want, discard what I don't, and never look back. Never, ever.

I tend to zigzag—live forward a while, then go backward and agonize over what might have been.

I dither over whether I should throw everything out and start over or whether I should backtrack and try to glue broken pieces together, tie baling wire around ripped-apart goods I never meant to throw away in the first place.

"Turn it off, Lovie. We've established that Thomas knew all the victims."

"What about motive? There might be something in these tapes to show why he'd want to kill them."

"What do you think? Thomas is going to make an appearance as their stud muffin?"

"Aunt Ruby Nell thinks he has the goods."

Holy cow. I hope not. Though the connecting door sends up all kinds of red flags, I'm still clinging to the hope that all Mama wants from Mr. Whitenton is his dancing feet.

"Lovie, we can't hole up in Thomas' room all day watching porn videos. Somebody's liable to catch us."

"Relax, Cal. It could enhance your reputation."

I know good and well what she means, but I choose to pretend otherwise. Everybody in Mooreville thinks I'm demure. Everybody except Jack. And he no longer counts. I think. I hope.

"My reputation's just fine, thank you very much. I'm the best hair stylist in northeast Mississippi. And that's not bragging. Everybody says so."

"Not *that* reputation."

Ordinarily, we'd engage in this kind of good-natured banter half the day, but I've got to get my crazy cousin moving. Besides, she's hitting a little too close to home for my comfort.

What if I do need to loosen up, roll with the punches, as Lovie is always saying? What if my love of routine and advance planning is one of the reasons Jack left me? As much as I'd like to think it was all his fault, I'm not that kind of one-sided, wrong-headed woman. I pride myself on being fair.

"Come on, Lovie. We'll take the tapes with us."

"Then what? Turn them over to the cops? Breaking and entering will probably get us thrown into jail. And I don't even want to think what they'll do to us for possession of stolen property."

"Especially since we still have Babs' purse. Holy cow, Lovie. We could even become suspects for the Peabody murders."

"Why didn't you say all that before we decided to go snooping?"

"Maybe we can make an anonymous phone call to tip off the cops about this stash."

"Later. We're just coming to the good part."

Lovie's so-called good part features scenes that make me want to remove every mirror from my bedroom. If I'd known intimacy could make you look like a contortionist monkey in a G-string, I'd have done it in the dark. Fully clothed. Without sound.

"Fast forward, Lovie. I don't think we're going to learn anything here."

"Speak for yourself."

"I mean, about *murder.*"

"Good Lord, Cal. You sound just like Rocky. I'll bet you haven't even let Champ find your national treasure."

"You're the one with the national treasure. Besides, Champ has lofty motives."

"There're only two motives worth mentioning, Callie. Chocolate and sex."

I like to think the human race is more evolved than that, but considering the things I've heard from women sitting in my beauty shop chair, I can see Lovie's point. In fact, I have enough anecdotal evidence to prove her point, but I'm not the kind of woman who goes around letting the sisterhood down by revealing tawdry secrets.

The real issue here is the DVDs. When these get in the hands of the press, sex and the Peabody murders will be spread all over the news. (Who knows? Maybe chocolate, too. We haven't seen all the DVDs yet.)

"Holy cow!" I dive toward the desk and start scooping up Mama's pictures. "Were there any more of these, Lovie?"

"What are you doing?"

"Stealing evidence. When this thing breaks, there's going to be a huge sex scandal, and these pictures put Mama right in the middle of it."

"None of them show Aunt Ruby Nell in a compromising position."

"Guilt by association, Lovie. Move your butt!"

She scrambles off the bed and barrels toward the desk. On the TV screen behind us, Gloria Divine and Latoya LaBelle carry on in ways that would send every Baptist in Mooreville into a prayer vigil.

Lovie and I rip into unopened envelopes, scattering pictures everywhere, including onto the floor. We drop to our knees and start snatching them up.

"Just get Mama. Leave the rest."

I make neat little stacks while Lovie stuffs pictures into the bosom of her uniform. Though how she has any room in there, I don't even want to guess.

"WHAT ARE YOU DOING?" Thomas' scream jerks me upright so fast, I bop my head on the underside of the desk.

Holy cow! How'd he get in? I'm sure I fastened the night latch. Is he a Houdini as well as a sex maniac and a killer?

"You!" he screams. "Get out of my room!"

Lovie's still scrambling around trying to get off the floor. Should I help her up or defend her?

I grab the lamp just as she rises to her knees. She takes one look at the madman storming our way and yells, "Balcony!"

The Peabody has no balconies.

By the time I gather enough wits to tell her, she's already halfway out the window. And Thomas is coming at a fast clip, an enraged senior citizen who has already killed three women and seems bent on killing me. I didn't know you could move that fast with a bandaged leg.

"Stay away." I brandish the lamp. "I'll use this."

There's a bloodcurdling scream. Is it Lovie, toppling to her death? Is it Thomas, coming in for the kill?

Or is it me?

All I know is that I swing the lamp. Hard. Thomas keels over like a felled giant redwood.

I'm too scared to kneel down and take his pulse. Besides, I don't know the first thing about CPR. All I know is that he's not moving.

I think I've killed him. Which is bad enough. But the worst part is, now my babies will be born in prison.

Elvis' Opinion #9 on Killers, Psychic Eyes, and Charm School

Stuck in the room again. If they think that's going to stop me, they might as well be singing "Heartbreak Hotel."

I sashay my ample self out of the closet. (Listen, I wasn't really pouting. I was just trying to teach Callie a lesson: how can a soul dog complete his mission if you keep leaving him behind?) Then I prance right over, grab the telephone by its cord, and drag it off the table.

If you think I don't know how to dial room service, you're barking up the wrong tree. How do you think I avoided being mauled by hoards of adoring fans? It was bad enough in the late nineteen fifties when my star was just beginning to rise. I couldn't sit down in a roadside restaurant without having girls all over my lap. After I was playing Vegas, I'd have been kidnapped and taken into love slavery if bodyguards hadn't whisked me out the back and up to my room.

You bet your blue suede shoes I know room service. Only trouble is, paws don't have movable digits. Fortunately, I'm not just another famous dog who howls with a drawl. I'm smart. If I can find a pencil, I'll have room service up here before you can say "T-bone steak."

Callie's left a pencil on the desk. Basset hounds may be God's gift to French poodles, but we've got stubby legs. If God had sent me back as a golden retriever, I'd be gnawing meat off the bone by now. As it is, I'm forced to rearrange the furniture. I'm in the process of overturning a chair to climb on when I hear the key in the lock.

I instantly go into *cute* mode. Callie will forgive anything if I flap my mismatched ears and put on a big doggie grin.

It's not Callie who comes through the door, though. It's Bobby Huckabee.

"What happened in here?" He puts the phone back on the table and picks up the chair. "Have you been a bad dog?"

Bad dog? Has he lost his tiny mind? Does he know who he's talking to?

Obviously he's immune to fame and charm. If I didn't need him for nefarious purposes, I'd hoist my leg on his shoes. Instead I put on a show. Contrite, hungry, lonely dog. Rescued, at last. Listen, I can act. If the Colonel hadn't pushed me into one shallow role after another, and had let me choose my own movies, there'd be an Academy Award in the Trophy Room at Graceland.

"I'll bet you'd like some food and some good company while you eat."

Well, now. There may be something to Bobby's psychic eye after all. He squats to scratch my ears.

"You know, I get so lonely eating by myself, I've started taking all my meals in front of the TV. Wheel of Fortune. It's like Vanna White is my best friend."

This man has some serious social issues. When we get back home I might have to teach him a thing or two.

While Bobby orders two fat hamburgers, I decide on the spot to become an entrepreneur. As soon as I get back to Mooreville, I'm opening a lonely hearts school. Listen, the King wrote the book on charm. If I can't teach Bobby Huckabee how to win French poodles and influence basset hounds, nobody can.

There's a loud rap on the door.

"Room thervice."

"Boy, that was quick."

Too quick. And that lisp is a dead giveaway. It's not hamburgers this dude is delivering. It's death.

I don't fancy lying in state again being mourned by millions. I've got too much livin' and lovin' to do.

Bobby is already headed to the door. I make an end run around him, then stand between him and the door. He'll cross my snarling, fat self at the risk of losing a limb.

Come on in, sucker. I dare you. I'm waiting for you.

Any minute now, I'm going to get my chance to be headline news. "Famous Basset Hound Foils Killer, Saves the Day."

Except for my growls of destruction and impending doom, all is quiet on the Western front. Has the killer vamoosed? Turned tail and run from my formidable presence?

Suddenly my mismatched ears perk up and my nose goes into overdrive. What's this I hear and smell?

Somebody raps sharply on the door. "Elvis. What's the matter, boy?"

My master calls.

I get my hackles under control so Bobby can let my human daddy in. Jack squats and rubs behind my ears and you might as well just add some jam and spread me on toast. Listen, if he'd do that to Callie, he wouldn't be in this divorce pickle.

"Did you see room service out there, Jack?" Bobby asks.

"Yes, but he was headed down the hall."

You bet your britches he was hightailing it out of here. Anybody with half sense and one eye would run if they saw Jack Jones looking like a cross between Indiana Jones and 007.

Jack glances around the room. "Where's Cal?"

"Looking for the Peabody killer."

"Any idea where?"

"I'm not getting a clear picture, but I think in her mother's boyfriend's room. And you'd better hurry. She's in danger."

Jack's out the door before Bobby can get the warning out of his mouth. Much as I'd like to go with him, there's a hunk of beef on the way. And my wind's not what it used to be. Just between you and me, I'm happy to see Bobby lock the door and wait for room service.

Chapter 21

Sex, Scandal, and the Resurrected Dead

Thomas Whitenton's still not moving. There's nothing I can do for him now, so I race to the window to rescue Lovie. Assuming she hasn't already plunged off the ledge.

Please, God. I'm praying every step. In the distance, sirens wail.

"Lovie," I call. "Are you all right?"

No answer. Just the screaming of emergency vehicles, the muted roar of a gathering crowd drifting up from the sidewalk ten stories below, and the sounds coming from the TV—Latoya LaBelle and Gloria Divine doing things I'd be embarrassed to tell you.

I'm drenched with sweat, I'm wearing concrete shoes, and somebody has moved the window. The Sahara lies between me and my cousin.

Suddenly sharp lights beam upward. God and his angels, come to escort Lovie to Glory Land? I move toward the light in slow motion.

"Lovie! Answer me!"

"No habla English!" she screams.

Good grief. Lovie has died and gone to . . . Mexico?

From ten stories below, an amplified voice floats up to the window. "Stand back. Everybody stand back. We've got a jumper."

Six years later and near heart failure (to say the least), I finally reach the window. A fireman is shouting to the crowd through a megaphone, eight more firemen make a circle around a vast net, and another sets up a ladder that could reach to kingdom come. Meanwhile, Thomas is expiring on the floor, Lovie's pinned in the lights of WCBI-TV, and cameras are rolling.

Could it get any worse? If I were the wrong kind of woman, I'd utter one of Lovie's improper words.

A pigeon swoops in and lands on Lovie's wig. Obviously he has higher aspirations, and is seizing his chance to end up on WCBI-TV's nightly news.

"Shoo, shoo." She jiggles around, flapping her arms, but the only thing that comes loose is the top button of her tight uniform. Photographs spill out and fly to the sidewalk like vivid birds. Mama, in various brightly colored caftans.

It just got worse. Tonight Mama will be all over the news. Lovie, too. If she lives that long. The ledge she's standing on is hardly big enough to hold the pouter pigeon on her head, let alone a hundred-and-ninety-pound bombshell doing the shimmy.

"Don't jump, lady," the fireman yells through the megaphone.

"No habla English!" Lovie yells back.

Maybe the black wig and the accent are enough to hide her identity for a while, but as soon as that sexy-looking fireman mounting the ladder reaches the top, Lovie's act as a voluptuous Mexican maid is history.

There's only one thing to do: rescue her myself.

"Hang on, Lovie. I'm coming."

I lean as far out the window as I dare and stretch my arms as far as I can reach. Behind me, Thomas has probably drawn his last breath and the dead erotic dancers are forever frozen on video, doing things I don't even want to know. If Lovie and I get out of this caper alive, I'm sending letters to God and Santa Claus and the president of the United States, to boot, apologizing for every one of my wicked deeds.

"Take my hand, Lovie. Inch this way and take my hand."

"If I move, I'll fall."

"No, you won't. One tiny step in this direction and I've got you." She shakes her head. No. I've never seen her speechless. "Come on, Lovie. You got out there. You can get back."

She shakes her head again while the fireman climbs closer and the shameless dancers grunt and groan on the TV screen in living color. And I don't even want to think about Mr. Whitenton.

I've got to get Lovie off the ledge and out of this room before we become bigger sensations than Elvis—the icon, not my dog.

There's only one thing to do: climb onto the ledge.

Sending petitions to God and Buddha and Mother Earth and deities I make up on the spot, I kick off my shoes and hoist one leg over the window-sill.

The megaphone-toting fireman yells, "Don't do it, lady. Stay back."

He might as well save his breath. I'm desperate enough to do anything. Including commit murder. Which I've already done. I try to look on the bright side. If I rescue Lovie in a spectacular act of selfless bravery, will the judge give me a lighter sentence?

Taking a deep breath, I reach for a protruding section of ornate concrete and prepare to hoist my other leg over. Suddenly, large hands circle my waist and I'm plucked off the windowsill.

"You never did listen to advice."

Jack Jones. Naturally. I don't know whether to kiss him or to slap his face.

He spins me around, rakes me from head to toe with the blackest, sexiest, most dangerous gaze in captivity, then drawls, "Kinky."

He pats me on the backside, then throws me over his shoulder and deposits me in the room's only wingback chair.

"Stay put. We'll play French maid and hungry rogue later."

I should have smelled him coming. All those pheromones. Not to mention the clean fresh scent of Irish Spring soap that clings to his skin no matter how long ago he took his shower. You know the scent. The one you could eat with a spoon.

Except I'm in no mood for eating Jack Jones with a spoon. Or any other way, for that matter. I'm scared and I'm mad. I've killed one man; I might as well kill two.

"Get Lovie off that ledge before I end your life."

What's happening to me? If I had time, I'd have a nervous breakdown.

"Yes ma'am." He winks, then disappears through the window.

If I were a vengeful woman, I'd wish he would fall. Fortunately I'm just a small-town hair stylist who wants a divorce so I can have a normal life, a normal husband, and lots of babies.

Plus, this is the first time I've seen Jack since I found out his profession. I feel dazed, blinded by truth. How could I have spent all those years dreaming in my marriage bed while my husband hid under dark bridges and blood-red moons, the body I kissed from head to toe both a target and a killing machine?

And now, he and Lovie could both die. Because of me. Because Jack wouldn't be here if I weren't involved, and I'm the one who wanted to prove Mr. Whitenton is a murderer.

Before I have time to work myself into a wad of weeping rage and guilt, Jack is back. With Lovie, thank goodness. Her wig's on crooked, she's got pigeon poop in her hair, and she looks like she just got her mojo back.

"Are you okay, Lovie?"

"I've just mooned Memphis on the six o'clock news. I should have charged admission." She buttons her blouse. "Why didn't you tell me this hotel didn't have balconies?"

"I was too busy killing Mr. Whitenton."

"You didn't kill him." Jack hauls Thomas off the floor. "But he has a lot of explaining to do."

"How'd he get in here?" I ask Jack. "I had the night latch on. For that matter, how'd *you* get in?"

"Connecting door." Well, naturally. Mama and Uncle Charlie were dancing, which means Mr. Whitenton picked the lock to her room and sashayed right in. What other locks has Mama let him pick?

On the big screen TV screen, Gloria and Latoya go into a particularly loud and embarrassing moment. Jack studies the screen and gets this amused look I'd like to slap right off his face.

"Your taste in movies has changed, Cal."

"Those belong to Mr. Whitenton," I tell him, and Mama's former dance partner turns the color of Lovie's hair. "It looks like we've caught the Peabody killer."

"Cal, I want you and Lovie to go to your room, lock up, and don't come out till I call."

Jack scoops up the DVDs, collars Mr. Whitenton, then vanishes. Which is just like him. I am glued to my chair with all the wind sucked out of me.

Lovie says one of her classic bad words, but I barely hear. I'm in the eye of a hurricane and can't get out.

"He didn't even acknowledge our part in collaring the perp," Lovie says.

At the moment, I'm not interested in the perp. All I'm interested in is getting enough oxygen into my lungs so I can breathe.

"Callie?" Lovie puts her hand on my shoulder. "Don't let him get to you."

"He's not. I won't." Is that a lie?

"Jack was always high handed. No wonder you can't live with him."

"Look on the bright side, Lovie. He took the DVDs off our hands. Now we won't have to deal with X-rated evidence."

"You don't have to defend him."

"I'm not." I brush my hair out of my hot face. "I'm just stating the obvious. That's all."

Lovie jerks off her wig, then mine. "Let's go to the room and get out of these maid outfits."

"But not to stay."

"Definitely not to stay. This show's not over till the fat lady sings."

Then Lovie stands right there in Mr. Whitenton's room and belts out "Hard Hearted Hannah." I guess she's trying to show me she's okay.

Or maybe she wants to remind me that soft hearts can get stepped on and tromped all over, that the best way to navigate life's treacherous tides and killing seas is to harden your heart. But not all the way. Just enough to stormproof it.

Chapter 22

Weddings, Breaking News, and Tequila

Lovie and I leave Thomas' room and make it to the elevator without encountering any needy guests requesting soap and shampoo or any nosey guests wondering why we're not riding the service elevator.

I punch the button for the fourth floor, and we both lean against the walls.

"I can't wait to get out of this uniform," I say.

"I can't wait for a drink."

"Anything except Long Island Ice Tea. I don't hanker for another tattoo."

"Live a little, Callie. We could get one that says 'I collared the Peabody killer.' "

"You really think Thomas did it?"

"Yeah. Don't you?"

"I don't know. Mama is usually astute about people. I can't believe she'd be so wrong about Thomas Whitenton."

"I thought you wanted him to be the killer."

"Not really. I just want him out of Mama's life.

Even if he's not a criminal, there's something about him that's just not right for her." Lovie rolls her eyes. "Well, he's not. He doesn't even appreciate Mama's Modigliani."

"That's not saying much, Callie. Neither does anybody else in Mooreville."

The door slides open, and I'm glad to end this conversation. We burst through and race toward our room, giddy with success.

Bobby and Elvis are sitting on the floor watching TV, two empty plates in front of them. The room smells suspiciously like hamburger.

When he sees me, Elvis thumps his tail and looks so smug, I don't have to have a psychic eye to know Bobby has been spoiling him.

"We caught the killer," Lovie announces.

"Who?" Bobby looks up from the TV, some show about Memphis' glitterati.

"Thomas," she says.

"We *think*." I scoop up the empty plates, then sit on the floor beside them. "We're going to celebrate. Do you want to join us?"

"You mean it?"

"Of course. Just sit tight while we change clothes."

"Here?" His face turns red.

"In the bathroom. You can stay put, or leave and come back. Your choice."

"Well, this show is interesting . . ."

"Hey." Lovie stares at the TV screen. "Is that Fifi Galant?"

"Yeah, it's a taped show. She's having her wedding rehearsal dinner at the Skyway tonight. How'd you know her?"

"I saw her picture in the paper." Lovie throws her wig in the direction of the closet and misses. I pick it up and put it on the top shelf. "I'd love to see the rehearsal dinner. I'll bet the Peabody's doing an ice sculpture."

"Maybe we can crash it," he says.

I can't believe it. Bobby? Crashing a wedding event?

He looks a bit sheepish, as if he's reading my mind. "I do that sometimes. When I don't have anything else to do. Which is pretty often."

"Let's do it, then," Lovie says. "I haven't crashed a party since college."

Leave it to Lovie. To give her credit, she is probably hoping to learn some new tricks for her catering business. Then again, her window-ledge high is wearing off. She could be just itching to get into more trouble.

"We will not be crashing any wedding parties. What we'll do is get out of these uniforms, stash them somewhere, then sit down and have a civilized drink. As long as it's not tequila."

"Maybe we can just scoot up to the Plantation Roof and peek into the Skyway."

"Hush, Lovie. Change your clothes. You can go first."

While she's in the bathroom, I sit on the floor and rub my dog's ears. Elvis leans against my leg and Bobby turns his full attention back to the interview with Fifi Galant. Frankly, I'm glad I don't have to talk to anybody or make plans to catch the killer or even think about anything. Especially about Jack and The Company and my divorce.

Closing my eyes, I try to get into a Zen-like state, fall into the moment and just *be*, but something on the TV catches my attention.

"We're having the wedding in the lobby of the Peabody," the bride-to-be is saying. "We'll be using the same red carpet used in the parade of ducks."

I snap my eyes open. What kind of weird person wants to drag her wedding gown down a carpet where ducks leave a nasty daily trail?

I stare at Fifi, something nibbling on the outer reaches of my mind. Why do I get the feeling I'm missing something?

I don't know why I do this—pick a subject to pieces even after the dust has settled and all the shouting is over. For goodness sake, we've caught the killer, solved the crime, closed the case.

Though Fifi is wearing subtle makeup and a subdued Albert Nipon dress, she still has an air of flamboyance, an unmistakable stage presence that almost screams *showgirl*. What did Lovie say? She got her start at Hot Tips?

Still, what does that have to do with anything? Except, two of the Peabody victims were showgirls. And both were killed near the fountain. Where the ducks swim.

"I'm finished." Lovie swings into the room in tight jeans and a hot pink tee shirt with a sequined cowboy across her awesome bosom, hot pink cowboy boots on her feet. "Make it snappy, Callie. I'm ready to rumble."

Relieved to be jerked out of my endless cogitation, I grab my clothes and head to the bathroom. If I could bottle Lovie, I'd mark her *Instant Personality* and sell her at Hair.Net for millions. She always makes me smile. Even better, she makes me forget what I was worried about in the first place.

After I change, Lovie and I stash the uniforms temporarily in our suitcases, then the four of us (including Elvis) head to Café Espresso in a row of little shops off the lobby. It has the old world charm of a Viennese bakery—terra-cotta floors, real linen napkins on the tables, a chef in white hat serving delectable edibles from a glass case. These pastries look so sinful, one mouthful could put twenty pounds on each hip.

Bobby selects a table for us near the Peabody promenade so that technically Elvis is not in the small eatery. Within minutes we're all deep in sugar-overload heaven. Even Bobby seems at ease.

"You know," he says, "Calls to God are local here. This is God's country."

"Amen," I say, and Elvis thumps his tail. Lovie has her mouth full and can't reply.

My cell phone shatters our peaceful outing. I don't recognize the number.

"Hello?" It's Jill. I never forget a voice. "Callie? I just wanted to let y'all know I'm home."

"Great. How's it going?"

"The minute I mentioned divorce, Mother started wringing her hands and Aunt Betty Jean started quoting scriptures." Jill giggles. "Then Mother saw my tattoo and nearly fainted."

"What'd you get?"

"Mine says 'Miss Paris Reigns.' I was on top of the world when I wore that crown and that's where I plan to be again. Nothing can stop me now."

"Good for you." I tell Jill about our escapades in Thomas' room while Bobby leans forward, all ears.

This is his first time hearing the particulars. "We're celebrating with pastries now."

"Have a fat flaky one for me."

"Will do."

"Callie? I can't thank you and Lovie enough for what you did for me. You two are my inspiration."

I don't think I've ever been anybody's inspiration. After Jill promises to keep in touch and says goodbye, I sit, in this quaint café, enjoying the good feeling of helping her find the right path, and collaring the killer.

"Who was that?" Lovie asks.

"Jill. She's great. Called us her inspiration."

"Thomas didn't do it." Bobby runs his finger around the bottom of his plate to catch an elusive pastry flake.

"What do you mean, he didn't do it?" Lovie's face is turning red with the effort to moderate her voice.

"I just had a vision."

"Visions don't mean squat in a court of law," she says. "We found evidence."

"Wait a minute, Lovie. I don't think the tapes are enough." Bobby's green eye is twitching but his blue one is staring across the promenade with a faraway look. How does he do that? "Tell us about your vision, Bobby."

"There's danger from a dark-eyed stranger."

"If you say that again, I'm going to scream." This from Lovie, who looks like she's about fifteen seconds from doing so now.

"Hush, Lovie. You're going to scare him." Keeping my voice low and even, I say, "What else, Bobby?"

"It's not personal," he says.

"What's not personal?"

"The murders."

"You mean he didn't mean to kill his victims, or he didn't know them?"

Bobby just sits there staring into space. Apparently, he's gone into some kind of trance.

"Why don't we just hold a séance right here in the Peabody? Maybe we can contact the victims and ask them."

"That's not nice, Lovie. Besides, people are staring."

"When I'm in the room, people always stare. I like to give them plenty to stare at."

Bobby still looks comatose and has now tilted sideways.

"Lovie, do you think he's going to fall out of his chair?"

"If he does, we'll just leave him here and pretend we don't know him." You could knock me over with a drop of tequila. Lovie's not mean spirited. "Just kidding, Cal."

"What are we going to do?"

"I don't know about you, but I'm going to order another raspberry pastry."

"What about Bobby?"

"I'll get one for him, too."

Lovie gets up and prances off. Which is just like her. If Bobby falls out of that chair while she's gone, I'm going to kill him.

Elvis' Opinion #10 on Rejection, Revelry, and Reformation

I can't speak for Bobby, but if Lovie doesn't bring a raspberry pastry for yours truly, I'm liable to take off somebody's leg. Listen, being on the sidelines is for untalented cocker spaniels. I may be a reformed former icon in a dog suit (meaning I can live without the spotlight as long as I get to rule over the oak tree where my ham bones are buried), but I'm no pushover. The only thing that can soothe my ruffled fur is food. And plenty of it.

What do they think I was doing up there in that room? Acting like a couch dog? I'm too full of piss and vinegar for that. Even though I was hampered by four walls and a watchboy (Bobby), I made every minute count.

Before Jack arrived, I got a good whiff of the killer at the door, and I can tell you right now: it's not Thomas Whitenton. If Callie would let me off this leash, I could track that scent down before you could howl "A Little Less Conversation."

Not consulting the King is enough to make a

lesser dog feel rejected. Of course, I'm not your average dog. Why do you think I get invited nearly everywhere Callie goes, including to the Café Espresso for their premature celebration?

For one thing, they have nothing to celebrate. But then, they don't know that, because they didn't bother to ask my opinion. For another, a pastry and a cup of coffee (water, in my case) are not what you'd call living high on the hog. If they want revelry, they ought to let me throw them a party in Graceland.

Now, there was some revelry. When I was living in Memphis, there was always a whole lot'a shakin' goin' on. Football in the back yard, target practice on the shooting range, and best of all, lots of good rockin' around the piano, with yours truly providing the accompaniment. I could still wrap my paws around the ivories if I had some digits.

These days, though, I'm lucky if I get to twang a few notes on Jack's guitar when I'm with my human daddy. Speaking of which, he's not going to be too happy that Callie's down here right in the path of danger.

Bobby's correct on that score. There's danger all around. Until Jack catches the Peabody killer, nobody's safe in this hotel.

Chapter 23

Disco Balls, Second Prize, and Second Guesses

My cell phone rings again, jarring Bobby out of his trance. It's Mama. Talking so loud you can hear her across the room.

"Callie, where are you?"

"Why?"

"Because you're not in this ballroom, and if you don't hurry, you'll miss the presentation of the trophies."

Holy cow. I forgot. Bobby and I round up Lovie, who has just paid for a second helping of raspberry pastries.

"What do I do with these?"

"Put them in your purse, Lovie. If we don't hurry, we'll miss seeing Mama and Uncle Charlie win a dance trophy." I glance at Bobby. "And don't you dare tell me they're not going to win."

I enjoy surprise. Unless, of course, it's Jack Jones surprising me in my own bedroom. In Mooreville and anywhere else he takes a notion.

We head through the lobby toward the Continental Ballroom just as the duck master is leading his feathered charges off the elevator. Elvis immediately takes offense. His hackles ruffle up and he starts that low, rumbling growl that means trouble.

"Elvis, no." I pull him in close to my left side. If he makes a scene, we could get thrown out of the hotel. A group of little old women having an afternoon toddy are already scowling in our direction.

"What's with Elvis?" Lovie says.

"He hates the ducks. You two go ahead. We'll catch up." I squat beside my dog and try to soothe his bad attitude with a Pup-Peroni treat from my purse.

Unfortunately, the duck master and his quacking entourage are headed in our direction. Elvis' whole body quivers. If he lunges, there'll be duck feathers all over the lobby. I grab his collar in a tight hold just as the duck master passes by.

No wonder my dog is taking umbrage. Surprisingly, that silly braid-trimmed jacket is buttoned up wrong and the bottom is hanging crooked. You'd think somebody who was getting ready to put on a show would at least get his clothes on straight.

Hunkered on the carpet with my quivering dog, I wait until the duck master passes, then hotfoot it toward the ballroom.

Mama is waiting at the ballroom door.

"What took you so long?"

"We got sidetracked by the ducks." Across the room, I spot Lovie and Bobby with Fayrene and Jarvetis. "Where's Uncle Charlie?"

"Oh, you know Charlie. Off on some wild goose chase."

"About what?"

"Jack's in town." She watches my face turn the color of a woman with one too many men and not enough willpower. "I see you already know."

"I do." Obviously Mama doesn't know that Jack and probably Uncle Charlie have escorted her former dance partner to the police station, and he's being booked for murder. If I tell her, though, it will spoil her day.

I lean over and kiss her cheek. "I hope you win, Mama."

"Oh, I will." As she leads me toward a row of chairs, she glances around the ballroom. "I wonder what's keeping Thomas?"

I have to bite my tongue to keep from telling her. Now is not the time for true confessions about a man whose hobby is porn videos. Not to mention murder.

Lovie and Bobby are waiting for us in the third row. In the second, Fayrene and Jarvetis are holding hands. It looks like Mooreville's answer to Lucy and Desi have completely made up. I'm glad. Without Jarvetis and his redbone hound, social life in Mooreville would never be the same. If he left, Fayrene would probably ditch the fish bait, and who would restock the shelves with pickled pigs' lips?

As I slide into the chair beside Lovie, I wonder why I'm not feeling a big sense of relief. We've caught the Peabody killer. Uncle Charlie's absence is verification enough. He would never leave Mama alone if he thought we'd nabbed the wrong man.

Of course, Jarvetis is here, and who knows?

Maybe Uncle Charlie told him to protect the ladies (those would be his precise words) until he returned.

I don't have time for further speculation, because the emcee is at the microphone in the center of the dance floor.

"Ladieees and gentlemennnn." He sounds like a ringmaster at a circus. When you think about it, though, this entire dance competition has had the feel of a Barnum and Bailey big tent show.

Acrylic trophies are lined in a glittering row on the table at the emcee's left. In the middle of the table beside a crystal vase of stargazer lilies sits the grand prize, a giant mirrored disco ball.

"How do they determine who gets the grand prize, Mama?"

"It varies with the competitions. In this one, it's judges' choice."

"What does that mean?"

"No rhyme nor reason, that's what it means. If they like you, you might get it. If they don't, forget it."

I pat Mama's hand. "I know they liked you."

"You think?"

"Who wouldn't, Mama?"

The way Mama's glowing, she looks like a teenager getting ready for her first date. No wonder Mr. Whitenton fell for her. I send silent prayers into the universe that she won't be too upset when he's charged with murder.

Suddenly, she grabs my arm. "That's me! That's me!" She jumps up and races toward the center of the dance floor.

I lean over and tap Lovie. "What did she win?"

"Didn't you hear? She and Daddy won the jitterbug competition." She glances around the ballroom, probably wondering the same thing I am. *Where is he? What could be taking so long?*

"Maybe there was a long line of criminals waiting to be booked," I say, and Lovie doesn't even look surprised. We've been reading each other's mind since we were kids. Just let us loose on the farm and we'd always head in the same direction, whether it was to our favorite oak climbing tree in the pasture or to the barn loft where we'd sit in the fragrant hay and dream for hours or to the lake where we'd watch the fish jump and make shining circles in the water.

Mama comes back with her trophy. "I'm going to build a special bookcase for this in the dining room."

"You already have a bookcase in the dining room."

"That's for books. This one will be for trophies. The first of many." She kisses her trophy. "Wait till Charlie sees this."

When the emcee holds up a trophy for the mambo and announces the award will go posthumously to Gloria Divine, a hush comes over the crowd. Gloria's partner, a slender, silver-haired man I'd noticed the first day of the competition, takes the microphone and gives a tearful speech.

"Gloria had a lifelong love of dance," he says.

Lovie punches me and I bite my tongue to keep from yelling. Not because of Lovie but because I've just remembered something. Fifi Galant, former exotic dancer and bride-to-be with her

Peabody fountain wedding, has the same last name as none other than the duck master. Melvin Galant.

I remember seeing his nametag when we were on the roof the evening Babs was pushed off. And most recently, while we were crossing the lobby and I kept Elvis from chewing off his leg.

What if Elvis knows something I don't? What if he had other reasons besides hatred of ducks to want to bite the duck master?

I'm fixing to grab Lovie and hightail it out of there when the emcee holds up the disco ball trophy.

"And nowwww for the Grand Prize! Winners are FAYRENE AND JARVETIS JOHNSON!"

Fayrene screams, then outruns Jarvetis and grabs the microphone.

"I'm prostate with joy," she yells, and the audience cracks up.

Jarvetis catches up with her and holds the disco ball trophy aloft. Fayrene clutches the microphone looking like she's getting ready to give a full-blown speech, but he escorts her off. Thank goodness. I don't think Memphis is ready for Mooreville's Mrs. Malaprop.

The disco ball was the final trophy and the audience is beginning to drift out of the ballroom. Soon a crew will be in here to strip, clean, and redecorate for this evening's Elvis tribute dance.

Giving Lovie the *look*, I offer quick congratulations all around, then the two of us head toward the door.

"We're going to splurge at Chez Philippe's," Mama says. "Aren't you coming?"

"I need to take Elvis out." I kiss her cheek. "Have fun."

"Wait. You can meet us later. I'll get a table big enough for all of us."

"You go ahead, Mama. Lovie and I will probably pick up a quick sandwich or something."

"What are you planning that does not include me?"

Mama gets this narrow-eyed look when she smells a rat. I'd hoped the trophy would take her mind off my business, but it looks like I'm wrong. Again.

"Aunt Ruby Nell, we'll see you at the dance tonight."

Mama rarely argues with Lovie. Don't ask me why. Maybe it's because they're so much alike— flamboyant, stubborn, maddening women who usually get their way.

Placated, she turns back to Fayrene, and the two of them start discussing how much money they're going to spend on dinner. Jarvetis just looks on with a half smile. Until the Memphis dance competition, I would have called that look *long-suffering*. Now I understand it's amused tolerance.

I pull Elvis up on a tight leash and am just heading toward the door and freedom when Bobby grabs my arm.

"I'll come with you."

"No need for you to miss the celebration. You go ahead with Mama."

His blue eye beams into mine. "There's danger."

Thank goodness, he didn't add *from a dark-eyed stranger*. I'm getting ready to tell him to have dinner with Mama and company when I remember the TV special he and Elvis were watching—all about dancer-turned-socialite Fifi Galant.

"On second thought, come with me," I tell him.

Bobby could know something that will help us find the real Peabody killer.

Chapter 24

Ice Statue, Icy Reception, and Flying Ice

When we get outside the ballroom, Lovie asks, "What's this about?"

"I think we got the wrong man." I tell them about the duck master's nametag.

"Could be coincidence," she says.

"No!" Bobby is usually quiet and rarely adamant. We stare at him. "Melvin Galant is Fifi's ex-husband."

"Are you sure?" Lovie thinks Bobby's psychic eye is balderdash (my word, not hers).

From time to time, she has also expressed serious doubts about his other mental capabilities. In private, of course. The only thing she's never disputed is his reputation as an undertaker. Like Uncle Charlie, Bobby can make the dead look like they're fixing to climb out of the casket and stroll down to Gas, Grits, and Guts for a Mountain Dew and a bag of boiled peanuts, cooked to perfection right in the parking lot. (Fayrene and Jarvetis like to keep a flea market going, weather permitting.)

"While you were snooping in the wrong room, Elvis and I saw this TV show where Fifi was saying she wanted to get married at the Peabody on account of her many happy memories here with her former husband. The duck master."

Lovie almost faints. First off, neither of us rarely hears Bobby utter more than six words strung together at one time. Second, she does not like to be told she did anything wrong. She's shocked at Bobby's not-so-subtle suggestion that she made a mistake going into Thomas' room.

Of course, I did, too, but I'm not as sensitive to criticism as Lovie. With Ruby Nell Valentine for a mother, how could I be? Of course, I mean that in the best way. Mama has taught me some wonderful life lessons. For one thing, *live large*. If I can master that, I think I'll be okay.

"Still," Lovie says, "that does not mean that Melvin Galant had a thing to do with the murders."

"Yes," I say, "but we have some strong connections. The showgirl angle plus the fact that all the murders took place around the ducks. And he was always there."

"What would be his motive?" Lovie asks.

"Bobby, did Fifi say anything else about Melvin?"

"Let me see. Just that his mother had been a showgirl. I think that was it."

"That's a lot of showgirls—the two Galant women and two of the victims." Elvis is straining at his leash, and I'm having a hard time standing in one place. "Still, how does Babs fit in?"

"And we still don't have motive. What's your plan, Cal?"

"Are you kidding me?"

"Well, you're the one who dragged us out here. You must have had something in mind." She grins. "Housekeeping, anyone?"

"Wipe that look off your face. We will not prance around this hotel again looking like French maid hookers in a bordello."

"I thought both of you looked very nice." Bobby blushes. "I mean. Really. You did."

"Thank you, Bobby. By the way, did you bring a computer?" He nods. "Why don't you check out the Galant family? If you find anything interesting, call my cell. And would you mind taking Elvis? Lovie and I may need to move fast."

"Okay. But maybe you should come with me. There's danger from a dark-eyed stranger."

"I know." I pat his hand. "Don't worry. I have Lovie."

Elvis is not happy to be leaving with Bobby. Like Mama, he loves to be in the middle of the action.

Lovie puts her hands on her hips. "You have me for what?"

"To go to the roof."

"No thank you. I've already seen the view. From the window ledge."

"We need to see what we can find out about Fifi and the duck master. Besides, I'm not asking you to climb over the balustrade."

"Believe me, I'm not planning to. What's our cover?"

I glance at my watch. The afternoon duck parade is over, so our timing should be perfect.

"You wanted to check out the catering for the wedding rehearsal dinner at the Skyway, didn't

you? We're crashing the party. Old friends of
Fifi's."

"Brilliant, Sherlock."

"If I don't get us both killed." A strong possibil-
ity. I'm beginning to have second thoughts.
"Maybe we ought to just call Jack or Uncle Charlie
and see if they booked Thomas."

"Daddy? Why?"

Holy cow. If I'm not careful, I'm going to have a
slip of the tongue and reveal Uncle Charlie's secret connection to The Company.

"Just because. Uncle Charlie always takes charge
of things. And Jack . . ." I shut my mouth before I
say anything else foolish. And dangerous. What
would happen if Lovie found out about The Company, and suddenly she slips up and tells Rocky
who just might tell his most trusted right-hand
man. All of a sudden, Jack's cover would be blown
and people all over the world could come gunning
for him.

And then where would I be?

Probably the same place I already am. In limbo.

"Come on, Lovie. Let's kick some serious backside."

"Lord, Cal. Why can't you just say . . ."

"I don't want to hear it, Lovie. What if I were
pregnant? Would you want your unborn niece or
nephew to come into this world using words like
that?"

"Probably not."

"See? So don't even say it."

"I'd wait till they were two to teach them."

Lovie's just kidding. I hope.

On the way to the roof, we stop at the fourth

floor to finish cooking our half-baked plan. While we're at it, Lovie takes the pastries out of the purse, then pops open a can of peanuts from her stash. I have to say the junk food is just what I need. We haven't had a real meal since this morning's brunch.

"Let's review, Lovie. So far, Thomas and Victor have been hauled in, so that leaves Grayson and now the duck master. Unless Thomas really is guilty."

"Don't forget Carolyn Mims."

"Okay, that's three viable suspects. There were no weapons, so every one of them had means, and they were all here, so that gives them opportunity." I nibble a peanut, hoping for inspiration. Nothing comes but the gut feeling that we're on the right track. "But the biggest piece of the puzzle is still missing."

"Motive. And don't forget, Cal, we could be dealing with more than one killer." Lovie finishes the last of her pastry, then digs into the can of nuts. "Did you bring your gun?"

"Are you kidding? To the Peabody? Besides, I've never hit anything except the side of a car and a very good pair of Jimmy Choo shoes."

Lovie disappears into the bathroom. I hear water running, then she emerges and pitches a damp washcloth in my direction.

"Here. Wipe the sugar off your hands."

"I could have washed them in the bathroom."

"Saves time. If we're going to blend in with the early arrivals at the wedding party, we've got to change clothes and we've got to hustle."

It doesn't take me long to slip into a simple

black sheath and sequined Manolo Blahniks. Not exactly the shoes I would choose for chasing a killer, but the black dress will be great for blending.

"Let's rumble." Lovie is standing in the bathroom doorway in a hot pink sequined full-skirted number that screams *see me*. Strike blending.

We head out the door, then trot to the elevator that will take us to the Skyway. Lord only knows what we'll do when we get there.

"Pray, Lovie."

"For what?"

"Divine invention."

She punches me and I punch her back. When all this is over, I hope we're still in a jocular mood. More to the point, I hope we're still alive.

It turns out Lovie was right about early arrivals. As we spill out of the elevator, we encounter a large group of tuxedoed men and perfumed women milling outside the Skyway. The flamboyant Fifi's friends. If their over-the-top eveningwear, à la Lovie, was not a dead giveaway, then the garish lipstick cinches the deal. Fifi's marrying a doctor. Trust me. These are not his cohorts. No doctor's wife would be caught dead in cheap lipstick.

A brassy blonde wearing tangerine approaches me. Somebody ought to tell her that shade of tangerine does not flatter her color type.

"Hi. I'm Janice. Are you a friend of the bride or the groom?"

"The bride. College roommate."

"I didn't think Fifi went to college."

"That Rosita." Lovie punches me on the arm. "Such a kidder." She winks at Tangerine Disaster, a.k.a. Janice. "She's a dropout of so many colleges, she thinks she got a degree."

I'm not sure Janice is buying Lovie's spiel. "Actually, I was surprised to get this invitation," I say. "Fifi and I haven't kept up and I haven't seen her in . . . like . . . *forever.*"

"Just between you and me, neither have I." Janice leans closer. "Actually, I've heard Fifi is pregnant, which, if you ask me, is the *only* way she could land a doctor."

"Does Melvin know?"

"Probably. I've heard he keeps pretty close tabs on Fifi."

"Odd," I say, hoping Janice will tell us more, but she's distracted by a guy with movie-star looks and no wedding ring. Excusing herself, she trots off after him.

"Come on, Cal. I see an ice sculpture."

We head into the Skyway. "Rosita?" I say, and she says, "Yeah, well, somebody had to think of something. We were going to be exposed before we ever got started."

The ice sculpture towers above the buffet table, a monumental art piece featuring two intertwined hearts surrounded by . . .

I can't believe my eyes.

"Lovie, tell me that's lovebirds."

"Look again. It's flying ducks. Carved in ice."

"Did Fifi love ducks that much or is she just rubbing Melvin's nose in her wedding?"

"Who knows? And what does it have to do with

murder, anyhow? I think we're barking up the wrong tree."

"Even if we are, just seeing this ice carving is worth being wrong."

"Since we're here, we might as well eat." Lovie grabs a plate off the end of the table.

"Put that back. We're not invited guests."

"Caterers always prepare extra. If we don't eat, a lot of this food will just go to waste." She piles chocolate petit fours on her plate.

"You mean go to *waist*."

"Cute, Cal." She hands one to me. "Eat this. You'll feel better."

Suddenly there's a small sound, like ice cubes breaking apart in a glass.

"Lovie? Did you hear that?"

"What?"

The sound comes again, louder this time. And it's coming from the direction of the bizarre frozen artwork. "That. Did you hear it?"

"Yes. It's . . . Oh . . . my . . . God. Run, Callie!"

Lovie's already streaking toward the door, leaving a trail of chocolate petit fours. I take off after her just as the ice sculpture explodes. Shattered ice crystals rain over my head and a chunk the size of the Portage Glacier, to say the least, narrowly misses my head.

If I don't watch out, tomorrow's headlines are going to read "Mooreville's Entrepreneur Killed by Flying Ice."

Chapter 25

Change of Plans, Who Dunnit, and Love Me Tender

My Manolo Blahniks are slipping and sliding on the ice. If I'm not careful, I'm going to join the women who are falling to the floor, their skirts flying over their heads like multi-colored kites.

I'm flailing my arms to keep my balance, but Lovie plows ahead like she has ice treads on her shoes. And she's not heading toward the door.

"Lovie. Wrong way!"

"I saw somebody."

"Who?"

"I don't know. He was wearing an Elvis mask."

We clear the icy portion of the floor and round the corner of the ladies' room. I see him now, just up ahead, racing down the hallway toward the kitchen wearing a mask with sexy, curled lips and black plastic sideburns. He's also wearing a suit with a double-breasted jacket trimmed in gold braid. If it's not the duck master, it's somebody wearing his suit.

"Melvin," I yell, and he turns to glance backward. "It's him, Lovie."

"I saw."

"Don't let him get away."

Our target picks up speed and slams into a waiter heading toward the Skyway with a loaded tray. Food shoots into the air, then crashes around us. I'm being buried under an avalanche of shrimp.

Undeterred, Lovie's gaining on the killer. The duck master ducks (no pun intended) into the service elevator and the door slides shut right in Lovie's face. I catch up, panting for breath and holding a stitch in my side.

Lovie says a word that would terrify small children and give old ladies heart attacks.

"We've lost him," I say.

"Not necessarily." She grabs my arm and drags me back up the hall. The poor, hapless waiter glares at us as if we've personally deprived the wedding party of shrimp.

"I'm sorry," I tell him, but I don't think it moderates his opinion of women who crash parties.

The only way to the public elevators is back through the Skyway, which is still in a high state of turmoil. Waiters are mopping up glass, tuxedoed men are trying to herd their dates to the ice-free corners, and women wearing cheap mascara are crying black tears. Nobody notices us.

Just as we reach the bank of elevators, my cell phone rings.

"Bobby? What do you have?"

"It's him, Callie. It's the duck master."

"Are you sure?"

"Positive. When he was three, his mother abandoned him at the stage door of the club where she worked, and you'll never guess what it was called."

"What?"

There's dead silence, and for a minute I think I've lost the connection. Then a new voice comes over the line.

"It was Club Hoochie Mama, Cal."

"Jack. Oh my God."

"Same to you, darlin'."

"Oh, hush." Why does this man always get under my skin? "The killer told Mama, *die, hoochie mama*."

"I know. We think Melvin went berserk after Fifi left, and started picking off dancers. He's still at large, babe. I want you to get your cute butt into your room and stay there. Take Lovie."

"You can kiss my big fat attitude."

"That's not what I plan to kiss, Cal."

The line goes dead. I'm so mad I could spit.

"What was that all about?" Lovie asks.

"Apparently Jack went looking for me and found Bobby and Elvis, instead. The good news is that Melvin Galant is our man."

I wouldn't be so certain if I had only Bobby's say-so, but Jack Jones always gets his man. At least, that's what Uncle Charlie told me. I tell Lovie the news about Melvin's mama.

"Great," she says. "Revenge is a big fat motive. If we're going to find him before Jack, we'd better hustle."

"Hustle where? Melvin Galant could be anywhere in this hotel. Shoot, by now he's probably on the streets."

"Remember his Elvis mask. Think of all the

hoochie mamas getting ready to fill the Continental Ballroom for the Elvis tribute dance."

"You think he'll show up? With cops all over this hotel, not to mention Jack Jones and the Valentine vigilantes?"

"Killers aren't governed by reason." The elevator arrives and Lovie punches the fourth floor. "I like *Valentine Vigilantes*, Cal. When we get home, let's have cards printed. VALENTINE VIGILANTES, GUNS FOR HIRE."

"Guns, my foot. We don't even have your baseball bat."

"Not for long." The elevator stops on the fourth floor and we get off. "I'm fixing to be armed and dangerous."

"You're always armed and dangerous."

Back in our room, we grab our Elvis masks as well as Lovie's weapon. Listen, a baseball bat might not sound like much, but in her hands it's as formidable as it was in the hands of Babe Ruth.

Still, this is not some juke joint. For goodness sake, this is the *Peabody*.

"Maybe we ought to rethink the bat. You can't go into the ballroom wielding that thing."

"Big skirts hide lots of things besides the Holy Grail and the national treasure. Besides, if Melvin Galant decides you're the next one who needs to die, you'll be glad I brought my lethal weapon."

Tucking the bat into the folds of her skirt, she heads out the door and I follow.

The ballroom is already filled with dancers. Usually I can spot Mama a mile away, but how can

I tell who anybody is with everybody wearing an Elvis mask?

"We'll never find him in this crowd," Lovie says.

I'm thinking she's right, when all of a sudden I see Bobby Huckabee standing in the doorway, mask in place, distinguishable from the crowd only by the dog he's holding on a leash.

"Oh yes, we will. Look who's standing in the door."

"Bobby? You've got to be kidding."

"No. Elvis."

"He's a pampered pooch, Cal. You think he can track?"

"He can smell Jarvetis' pickled pigs' lips from across the street and Ann-Margret halfway across Mooreville. You bet your sweet patootie he can track."

"Brilliant, Sherlock."

"Thank you, Watson."

I whip out my cell phone and ring Bobby's number. "Stay put, Bobby. Lovie and I are headed your way. We need Elvis."

"Doesn't everybody?" Bobby says.

I can never tell whether he's kidding. Though I'm finding out there's more to Bobby Huckabee than meets the eye.

He's so glad to see me, he wags all over himself. (Elvis, not Bobby.) I squat beside him and rub his ears (my dog's, not Bobby's).

"How would you like to sniff out some dastardly ducks, boy? Ducks?" He wags his tail, but I'm not a hundred percent sure he understands what I'm saying. "I wish we had some duck feathers."

"There's bound to be some in the fountain," Bobby says. "I'll go see."

"Thanks, Bobby. We'll wait here."

"By the refreshment tables," Lovie amends.

As Bobby leaves, Lovie makes a beeline for the food. Keeping Elvis on a short leash, I strike out after her, but I can't plow straight through the crowd without getting my dog trampled. Looking for openings, I meander.

Suddenly Elvis pulls against the leash. Hard. I'm getting ready to play our usual tug of war and test of wills when I notice he has his nose to the floor.

My dog is on the scent. Let's just hope it's not the scent of beef shish kebabs.

"Get 'em, boy. Sic 'em." A few heads turn my way, but if people are glaring, I can't tell because of the masks.

Letting Elvis take the lead, I'm pulled away from the refreshment tables and across the room toward the stage. Too late, I realize I'm losing Lovie and her baseball bat.

"Lovie," I call, but over the buzz of conversation, she doesn't hear me.

The stage is at the center back of the ballroom, approximately fifteen feet wide and eight feet deep. Onstage, band members are setting up their snare drums and electric guitars. An Elvis look-alike in a red jumpsuit covered with rhinestones fiddles with the microphone.

Holy cow. Is my dog heading this way to steal the show? It would be just like him.

The drummer hits a few licks and the faux Elvis breaks into "Heartbreak Hotel," which describes the current state of the Peabody to a tee. Ask any of the victims.

Not to mention my torn-to-pieces self.

Elvis lifts his head and howls. Fortunately, nobody notices. They're all on the floor gyrating to the beat. Plus, the music is loud enough to burst eardrums.

Hot on the trail, Elvis vaults onto the stage, with yours truly being dragged along for the ride. The Elvis tribute artist sees my dog and grins. I'll bet he thinks we're part of the act. After all, the King once sang to a basset hound on the "Steve Allen Show."

Elvis flies past the drummer and knocks over the cymbals. They crash to the floor, but the band never misses a beat. And neither does my dog. He's streaking backstage.

I fly through the curtains after him. And straight into the arms of the duck master.

"Your turn to die, hoothie mama."

In one smooth move, he wraps a scarf around my neck. I can't yell. I can't breathe.

"Heartbreak Hotel" plays on while the masked audience stomps and claps. The duck master tightens my noose.

Where's the baseball bat when I need it? Where's Jack? Where's Lovie? Probably eating cake while I am going to die.

The leash goes slack in my hand and Elvis breaks free. He lunges and the duck master screams. The scarf drops to the floor and I gulp for breath.

Sucking air into my starved lungs, I stagger

backward. Elvis has Melvin Galant's leg in a death hold. He's shaking the duck master like a cotton-mouth moccasin on Mama's farm that he's planning to kill.

"Cal!"

It's Jack, racing to my rescue. Thank goodness, I'm no longer the kind of woman who needs rescuing. I kick off my Manolo Blahniks, pick one up, and whack Melvin over the head.

The spike heel draws blood and the Peabody killer slides to the floor. Elvis takes one look at my attacker, lifts his leg, and pees on Melvin's shoes.

I'm going to buy him a T-bone steak for supper.

"Elvis, you're my hero."

How I ended up in the honeymoon suite of the Peabody would be a mystery to me if I didn't know Jack Jones so well. After all the shouting was over and Melvin was led away in handcuffs, Jack just whisked me off.

And I was too shaken to protest. At least, that's what I'm telling myself.

I'm also telling myself that in spite of the fact that Jack has kissed the bruises on my neck and is now kneeling beside the loveseat massaging my ice cold feet, I will not let him see my unicorn.

"I don't care what you do, Jack Jones. I'm keeping my clothes on."

Famous last words. Fifteen minutes later he's peeling me like an onion. When my dress hits the floor, he starts laughing so hard I figure he's finally coming unhinged. If I'd kept umpteen secrets from my spouse, I'd come unglued, too.

"What?" I say. "What?"

"A unicorn tattoo. I can't believe it."

He goes off into another gale of guffawing, which serves the wonderful purpose of bringing me to my senses.

Scooping my dress off the floor, I cover my unicorn.

"Jack. I want a divorce."

"I can see that. You've got our love symbol tattoed all over your cute butt."

"I'm serious, Jack. I want children."

"We've gone through all that, Cal. The time's not right."

I'm not fixing to get into another argument with Jack about timing while my eggs atrophy. I'm determined to end this once and for all.

"The time's never going to be right for you, Jack. I know what you do. I know what The Company is."

He crams his hands into his pockets and walks to the window.

"Fine," he says.

"Fine?"

"I'll sign the papers."

I can hardly believe my ears. This is what I want. Isn't it?

"You'll sign?"

"Yes. You can have whatever you want."

"You won't fight me for custody of Elvis?"

"No."

He turns back around and strolls my way, smiling. If I didn't know better, I'd swear he was wearing a mask.

"Maybe you'll name the first kid after me, Cal."

You can hear my free-at-last eggs shouting hal-lelujah all the way to the Mississippi River.

"Maybe I will, Jack."

He doesn't hear me. He's already out the door.

I stand in the middle of the honeymoon suite picturing myself adding a playpen to Hair.Net.

Elvis' Opinion #11 on Stardom, Freedom, and Being a Hero

Everybody's back in Mooreville now, and according to my human mom, everybody's happy.

I could say that would be true about everybody except Callie.

Lovie's got a ticket to join Rocky down in Mexico. Nobody's said exactly where he is. Just somewhere in the jungle digging up old bones. A man after my own heart.

I might see if I can finagle a ticket for myself. Digging is one of my specialties. Second only to turning the music world upside down and solving crimes. Listen, who do you think nabbed the Peabody killer?

If it hadn't been for my sharp nose and even sharper teeth, he'd probably still be running around Memphis killing hoochie mamas. I knew it was him the minute I smelled him coming down the hall while Callie and Lovie were stealing maid outfits. A trained hound dog never misses the scent of eau de duck.

As for the rest of the Valentine clan, Ruby Nell's content to have her guardian angel back. She and Charlie haven't crossed swords since we got back from Memphis. In fact, he's agreed to be her dance partner now that Thomas Whitenton is out of the picture.

Though Thomas was released from jail, he's one thing Callie will no longer have to worry about. The minute Ruby Nell found out her light-footed partner had a secret taste for porn, she dismissed him from her life. Permanently. Listen, Ruby Nell may act like a wild woman who loves getting on Callie's last nerve, but she's got nearly as much sense as a basset hound. If somebody would put her on the ticket for president, I'd vote for her.

And speaking of Mooreville's glitterati, Fayrene and Jarvetis have added a new attraction over at Gas, Grits, and Guts. The disco ball dance trophy is on display right beside the pickled pigs' lips. Fayrene even had Jarvetis install a special overhead spotlight. You can't walk into the store now without seeing mirrored rainbows all over the peas and corn.

They're even over the fish bait. Some of the diehard fishermen are turned off by shiny fish bait, but give them time. Jarvetis and Fayrene are icons around here. Moorevillians may be slow to adjust to the dancing disco ball, but they'll come around.

There are other big doings across the road, too. The minute I gave my old pal Trey the all-clear signal, he meandered on home. Jarvetis woke up one morning and found his favorite redbone hound sitting in the kennel waiting for his Purina Dog Chow.

And Fayrene's hired a construction crew. Work has already started on Bobby's séance room. He's so happy, he's stopped predicting *danger from a dark-eyed stranger.*

Back to my human mom.

Don't let her smile fool you. Even though she's acting like she's jumping for joy over Jack's promise to sign divorce papers, I can smell her sadness a mile away.

Listen, I know her better than anybody. She used to keep the radio on all the time at Hair.Net. She'd tap her foot to the beat while she cut hair, prance around while she was folding towels, sing along if she knew the words. She'd even whistle while she mixed that dratted perm solution that smells like dead rats even a dog wouldn't touch.

These days, she spends a lot of time squatted beside me rubbing my ears.

"It's okay, boy," she'll say, but I don't think she's trying to reassure me. If you want my opinion, she's trying to reassure herself.

She'll stop right in the middle of rolling Fayrene's hair and gaze out the window, her head tilted. I know what she's doing: listening for the sound of Jack's Harley Screamin' Eagle.

Jack's not coming. I could tell her, but there's no use driving a stake through her heart. He's holed up in his apartment, which smells like dirty socks, congratulating himself that he's doing the right thing. Now that he understands Callie's bone-deep need for children, he thinks signing the papers is going to make her happy.

Listen, neither one of them wants this divorce. If Jack Jones signs the papers, I'm a Chihuahua. And we all know Mexican food gives me a bad case of heartburn.

Don't hold your breath, is all I've got to say.

Meanwhile, there's a foxy Frenchie down the road who is hot to see her hunk'a burnin' love. Not to mention five of the smartest puppies who ever called a King *daddy*.

I sashay my heroic butt through the doggie door and walk around the perimeter of the back-yard fence. A dog of my intelligence can always find an escape route.

Thank you. Thank you very much. Elvis has left the building.

It's two times the turmoil for mayhem magnet Callie, her curvaceous cousin Lovie, and Elvis, the King reincarnated as nothin' but a hound dog. This time they're finding a lot more than relics on an archeological dig that could truly be their ruin . . .

Forced to choose between one man who wants to marry her and another who already did, Callie Valentine Jones can't think of a better way to check out of her personal Heartbreak Hotel than to get way, way out of town. So when Lovie invites the whole Valentine clan to visit her brainy new beau's work site near Cozumel, Callie packs up her crooning basset hound and heads straight for the airport.

But the moment they arrive at the dig, Elvis sniffs out T-R-O-U-B-L-E, in the form of a skeleton too fresh to be part of the research and too dead to spell anything but homicide. Suspicious minds blame ghosts and gods, but Callie knows the guilty party is all too human—and for once, she's determined not to get involved.

That determination goes right out the window when Lovie and Elvis go missing. It's now or never, if Callie wants to save her cousin and her canine from someone who's got murder always on his mind. And when her sexy ex arrives to save the day, she'll have to keep her head together, because her love won't wait—but neither will a killer with something deadly to hide.

**Please turn the page for an exciting sneak peek of
ELVIS AND THE TROPICAL DOUBLE TROUBLE
coming next month!**

Elvis' Opinion #1 on the Valentines, Manicures, and Mooreville's Royalty

Ever since I used my famous nose to crack the Memphis Mambo Murder Case, things have gone to the dogs around here. And I don't mean to a musical genius in a basset hound suit, either. (That would be yours truly.)

To hear my human mom (that would be Callie Valentine Jones, owner of the best little beauty shop this side of the Mason-Dixon Line) tell it, life just couldn't get any better. She thinks she's happy since she said "The Last Farewell" to Jack (my human daddy) up in Memphis, but I know better. When she's not giving New York hairdos to Mooreville's finest and doling out the dough for her mama's little gambling escapades—and every other kind of escapade Ruby Nell Valentine can think of—she's sitting on the front porch swing with a faraway look in her eyes that says, "Stuck on You."

Listen, I know she believes Jack is finally going to give her a divorce so she can have her heart's desire with somebody who won't spend more time in the world's underbelly avoiding bullets than he does in the gazebo with Callie and her "Ain't nothin' but a hound dog" best friend. (I'm not even going to talk about Hoyt, that ridiculous cocker spaniel pretender to my throne, and the seven silly cats who took up residence with us when Callie rescued them and dragged them home.)

Believe me, Jack's face said it all when Callie and the rest of our gang headed home from Memphis—"There Goes My Everything." A man that smitten is not going to let his woman go, no matter how noble he thinks the gesture might be.

I'm trying to teach Jack and Callie to be thankful for what they've got—each other plus a suave, famous Rock 'n' Roll King who is content to live a dog's life in order to make his humans happy. Instead, they're intent on turning everything upside down to get what they think Callie wants. A child. Someone just like the short, not-too-bright little person who makes car noises all day long, smears peanut butter on my pink satin guitar-shaped pillow, pulls my mismatched ears, runs Tonka trucks up the legs of Callie's customers, and generally has turned everything upside down here at Hair.Net.

This particular little person is David. He was part of the package when his mom, Darlene (Callie's new manicurist), moved in lock, stock, and uppity Lhasa apso.

That would be William, who claims he's the Dalai Lama reincarnate. He's prancing around here, even as I speak, acting like he outranks the King. I thought he'd get the message when I howled "The Great Pretender," but he just did his silly Lhasa flop that made Callie say, "Isn't he the cutest little dog?"

Cute, my slightly crooked hind leg. "Don't step on my blue suede shoes" is what she ought to be saying. That silly fuzzball's motto is "Rip It Up."

Mine is "Suspicious Minds." Listen, you can't trust a dog with a bushy tail. What's the use of a tail that can't point to rabbits? Or thump the floor like a drum? Or whack your human mom's legs to let her know you love her?

Wait till Callie finds out William sneaked into the beauty shop closet and chewed the toe out of her favorite Steve Madden moccasins. She loves her designer shoes.

But even with that dumb dog chewing up everything in sight and trying to steal my spotlight, and with David trying to pull my tail, I have to admit business has picked up around Hair.Net. Ever since Fayrene's daughter moved back home with her entourage (which includes a cat named Mal, which I'm not even going to dignify with a comment) and started dispensing Atlanta nail art, we've been booked to the hilt. Everybody who is anybody comes here to have Darlene paint witches and pumpkins on their toes. And while they're at it, they end up getting a new hairdo for Halloween.

Business is popping over at Gas, Grits, and Guts, too. People have been coming from Mantachie and Saltillo and even as far off as Red Bay, Alabama, to admire Fayrene and Jarvetis' disco ball dance trophy. They hung it over the pickled pigs' lips, then proceeded to spotlight it so it would send rainbows over the Vlasic pickles and Lay's potato chips. My best friend, Trey (Jarvetis' red-bone hound), tells me that Fayrene and Jarvetis (Mooreville's answer to royalty) are acting like lovebirds these days in spite of the fact that work is progressing on the séance room he said she'd build onto the back of their convenience store over his dead body.

And speaking of dead bodies... ever since Charlie Valentine thought Ruby Nell was going to join the body count during the Memphis Mambo Murders, he's back to being her best friend as well as the backbone of the entire Valentine family. As a matter of fact, he's planning to take her to the undertakers' convention in the Yucatan.

That leaves only one Valentine unaccounted for—Lovie, Callie's 190-pound, over-the-top flamboyant cousin. Currently she's in the Yucatan at Rocky's archeological dig promoting an agenda that features the love of her life discovering her "national treasure." She had that tattooed on her bombshell hips when we left off trying to catch a killer long enough to have a little fun up on Beale Street in Memphis. Personally, I think the "national treasure" ought to be added to the list of world wonders.

Here comes that five-year-old, pretending he's a Peterbilt rig. I'd escape through the doggie door and mosey on down to see what's cooking with my cute Frenchie (that would be Ann-Margret) and my five handsome progeny, but somebody has to keep things straight around here. Ruby Nell will be here any minute. She called to say she wanted to get spiffied up for her trip, but you can bet she's up to something. And I'm just the dog to find out. These mismatched radar ears miss nothing.

Well, bless'a my soul. The little person is carrying a cone of vanilla ice cream. That goofy Lhasa just waves his useless, ostentatious tail, but I know opportunity when it knocks.

I heft myself off my cushion, hum a few bars of "(Let Me Be Your) Teddy Bear," then mosey on over to see if the short person will let me lick ice cream off his elbows.

Chapter 1

Mooreville Gossip, Mexican Capers, and Misbehaving Mamas

Mooreville was edging toward fame with the disco ball dance trophy at Gas, Grits, and Guts, plus my dog Elvis, who thinks he's the King of Rock 'n' Roll. But I put it on the map when I hired an Atlanta manicurist who paints roses with faux jewels—and everything else you can imagine—on my customers' nails. My little beauty shop is now the talk of northeast Mississippi.

When I hired Darlene Johnson Lawford Grant to enhance the beauty experience of my clients at Hair.Net, I never figured on getting another menagerie plus a cherub / holy terror on chubby, dimpled legs. (Her son, David, from what Darlene terms her "second and final" marriage.)

Not that I'm complaining. In fact, just the opposite. Having a five-year-old running around the shop is almost like having my own little boy. Now that Jack Jones has promised a divorce and Luke Champion is acting like he's my personal prize stallion (he's a vet, which explains the animal analogy), I see my most cherished goal—mother-hood—just over the horizon.

The only hitch is that I keep seeing my aspiring stallion-in-hot-pursuit as a delicious-looking blonde confection you admire through the window, but never get the burning desire to reach in and take a bite of.

On the other hand, just let my almost-ex come within spitting distance, and I want to eat him up, starting with his dark, always mussed hair and ending with his size twelve feet, which just about says it all.

But where Jack's concerned, I've decided to make *no* my new middle name. After all, everybody in the know in Mooreville's society considers me an entrepreneur on the upswing since Hair.Net got a manicurist. I'd be featured in the newspaper if Mooreville had one. Which is not likely in the next fifty years, considering Darlene and David are the biggest population explosion we've had in ten years. And they only brought the live body count up to six hundred fifty-two.

Holy cow, listen to me, thinking in body counts. I'm turning over a new leaf. Now that we've put the Peabody murderer behind bars, I'm giving up crime. Period. Unless you consider it criminal to amass the stash of cash I'm saving so I can hit the after-Thanksgiving shoe sales next month.

The sight of Mama in her red Mustang distracts me from thoughts of cute designer shoes. She's driving with the top down. Anybody else her age would drive with the top up. Shoot, they wouldn't even have a convertible in the first place. But that's Mama, sassy all over, and I have to say I'm glad. In this day and age, a little joie de vivre can take you a long way past the blues.

Mama's wearing a flaming red caftan which matches her car, but clashes with her hair. I might tell her, depending on what kind of mood she's in. She doesn't always take criticism well, even if it's well meant. Which mine most certainly is. My motto is *Be nice to everybody*. There's too little kindness in this world, and I try to do my part to spread it around.

Mama bursts through the front door and charges in like she owns the place. "I want the works."

"Mama, whatever happened to *hello?*"

"Flitter, everybody here knows who I am." Mama sashays over to the manicure table to see what color Darlene is painting Fayrene's fingernails. "Is that green?"

Well, naturally. Fayrene always decks herself out in the color of money.

"It's called peacock." Fayrene holds up her left hand. "It matches the new swimsuit cover-up I bought for my trip to the undertakers' convention."

For once Mama is speechless. If I recall, she never invited Fayrene, even if they are best friends.

"You didn't think I'd let you go to Cozumel without me, did you, Ruby Nell?" Fayrene blows on her left hand, though she knows good and well I've installed the latest technology, a nail dryer in pink, which happens to be my signature color, as well as Elvis' (my dog *and* the real King). Plus, it matches my loveseats with the hot pink vinyl covers.

"Besides," Fayrene adds, "that hammering over

at Gas, Grits, and Guts is driving me crazy. As much as I want a séance room, I need some rest and respiration."

Relaxation, I hope, but you never can tell. Maybe Fayrene's having breathing problems I don't know about. Which is highly unlikely. The grapevine in Mooreville is alive and well. Not that I gossip. Far from it. But I pride myself on having created a spa-like atmosphere in Hair.Net. (That's why I painted a beach scene on one wall.) I want my customers to be totally relaxed and to feel free to tell me everything.

"Mother's horoscope said she'd be traveling to hot climes this month." Darlene consults the stars daily. I didn't know this when I hired her, but I was tickled pink to find it out. Any woman in touch with the stars is a welcome addition to Hair.Net.

Besides, Darlene's a natural blonde with flawless skin and thick hair cut in long layers, perfect for her pretty little heart-shaped face. With her angelic looks and unflappable personality, she's drawing customers in here like there's no tomorrow. Even the men are abandoning the Mooreville Barber Shop to come here for a great cut from yours truly and a good gander at Darlene in her slim-cut jeans and Texas style, genuine alligator-skin boots. She and Lovie have a lot in common.

The last two days, though, Darlene's been looking a bit frazzled. I can't help but notice how relieved she looks that her mother is talking about leaving the country.

Currently Darlene, her son, and their menagerie are living with Fayrene and Jarvetis. I guess they're feeling a little crowded over there. That will happen after about a week of company. And I know for a fact she's already been with her parents for three weeks.

My next project is to help Darlene find a little house with rent she can afford.

Darlene's unfazed when Mama plucks some Persian pink polish right out from under her nose, then proceeds to open the bottle and paint her own nails.

"Mama, if you'll care to remember, Darlene's the manicurist. Besides, that color clashes with your caftan."

"Since when is it a crime to try out a nail color in my own daughter's beauty shop? And for your information, if I want beauty advice, I'll ask for it."

As if that didn't announce her mood loud and clear, Mama flounces into my chair, snatches up a hand mirror, and views the back of her head like it's the burning of Chicago and I've personally lit the torch.

"I can't do a thing with my hair. You made a mis-whack the last time."

"That's not even a word, Mama. And even if it was, I never miswack."

I cinch the haircutting apron around her neck a little tighter than usual. Listen, I may be a pushover when it comes to Jack and babies and Elvis and stray cats and dogs—well, to just about everything—but I have my limits. And being called anything less than a total expert with hair is one of them.

I'm so good, my older customers make post mortem hair appointments while they're still alive. I have a whole shelf devoted to the special color blends I use on some of my customers (Bitsy Morgan and Mabel Moffett, to name two) in case I'm out of current stock if they die unexpectedly and need a little touch-up.

If you're wondering, I also fix up hair and makeup of the deceased over in Tupelo at Uncle Charlie's Eternal Rest Funeral Home.

"What do you want me to do today, Mama?"

"Take an inch off, color me jet black, and loan me about five hundred."

There goes my after-Thanksgiving shoe shopping spree.

"Holy cow, you'll only be gone a few days."

"It's for incidentals."

"How many incidentals can you buy, Mama?"

"You never know. I hear Cozumel is a shopper's paradise. I might need six hundred."

At this rate, I'm going to have to go to the Yucatan to keep up with my money.

Besides, Mama's not going to like her hair black. Knowing her, she'll get a thousand miles away, then call me to fly down and turn her into a redhead.

"Black's too harsh for your face, Mama."

"It's my hair. Besides, while I'm south of the border, I want to look like a señorita."

"There's no use arguing with Ruby Nell." Fayrene prances over, plops herself into the empty chair next to Mama, then proceeds to hold her hands out to admire her green nails. "Every time I argue with her, it just irrigates the tar out of her."

Nobody raises an eyebrow. Around here, we're used to Fayrene's rearrangement of the English language.

"Still, it's my job as a hair professional to steer my customers to a flattering color."

"Carolina, I'm not a paying customer." Mama always calls me by my real name when she's mad, though I can't think of a thing I've done to get on her bad side except continue divorce proceedings with Jack Jones. She thinks he walks on water. "I don't know if I want to go jet black or raven."

The phone rings and I'm relieved to abandon my losing battle over Mama's disastrous hair choice. Lovie's name pops up on the caller ID.

"Callie, is the speaker on?"

"You don't have to shout, Lovie. I can hear you. And, no, the speaker's not on."

"Turn it on. I want everybody in Mooreville to know what's going on down here."

"Don't you even want to know who's in the shop?"

"I don't care. I need some love advice. The more the better."

"Hang on."

I might as well turn the speaker on. Mama's leaning over so far trying to eavesdrop, she's about to fall out of her chair. Plus Fayrene and Darlene are all ears.

I'm glad I don't feel the need to spread around my love life, or the lack thereof since Jack walked out. But my cousin enjoys being a one-woman show. She says it's good for business (she's the best caterer in the South), but personally I think she's just trying to cover up that big soft heart of hers, which makes her open her arms—and other body parts I'm too much of a lady to mention—to anybody who needs a dose of "Love Me Tender."

That's one reason I'm pulling so hard for Rocky Malone. He's the first man who has ever treated my cousin like the treasure she is. Besides, he's the kind of gentleman who would take good care of a woman. Plus, he's a very fine archeologist with a good shot at becoming world-renowned if things go well at his Mayan dig.

I put the phone on speaker. "You can broadcast to the masses now, Lovie."

"We've got everything down here—romantic sunsets over the water, a lovers' moon over the Mayan ruins, privacy out the wazoo—and Rocky's not even close to discovering the national treasure."

"I thought he was searching for a lost city," Fayrene says.

"It's the lost tomb of the Nine Lords of the Night," Lovie tells her.

Mama chimes in. "The national treasure is my niece's *you know what,* Fayrene. She had it tattooed."

"Where?" Darlene wants to know.

"In Memphis," I tell her, but Lovie says, "On my hips, one word on each. About as close to the Holy Grail as you can get."

"The Holy Grail?" Fayrene looks puzzled, and her daughter says, "Mother, don't ask. I'll tell you later."

"I've tried everything," Lovie says. "When I went skinny dipping, Rocky ran to get me a bathrobe. And the only rise my Dance of the Seven Veils got out of him was to get up and turn down the lights in case somebody was looking in the window."

"I think that's sweet, Lovie," I tell her. "Rocky's an old-fashioned gentleman." Something my almost-ex never was.

Lovie says a word that should not be broadcast over the speakerphone.

Here I am doing everything I can to reassure her, when Fayrene pops up with, "Got any cards? I used to play strip poker with Jarvetis."

I don't even want to picture that.

I'm thinking this whole speakerphone conversation was a bad idea, when little David wanders into the room trailing Elvis. Could it get any worse? Now I'm a party to polluting the mind of the innocent, plus my dog has ice cream all over his muzzle. Thank goodness, Darlene jerks up her son and whisks him to the back room.

"Flitter, Fayrene," Mama says. "Anybody can play strip poker. Try a little lap dance, Lovie."

I don't even pretend her suggestion shocks me. Ever since I saw Mama doing the mambo up in Memphis with Mr. Whitenton, nothing shocks me where she's concerned. Though I'm happy to report that after she found out Thomas Whitenton was not the gentleman we first thought, she hasn't invited him back to her farm. Or any other place that I know of. Unless she's keeping secrets. Which she's perfectly capable of doing.

"Aunt Ruby Nell, when are you and Daddy flying down?"

"Day after tomorrow, Lovie. Charlie wants to have plenty of time to tour Rocky's dig at Tulum before the undertakers' convention."

"That's great. Callie, why don't you come?"

I'm just getting ready to say *I can't leave Hair.Net* when Mama says, "Fayrene's coming, too. By the time we get there, we'll have a seduction strategy."

Holy cow! This trip has disaster written all over it. When it comes to a choice between taking care of business in Mooreville and preventing Lovie from implementing Mama's seduction strategy in the Yucatan, there's no contest.

"I'll be there, Lovie."

My dog prances by, looking miffed. I swear, he acts like he thinks I ought to buy him a ticket, too. Which is perfectly ridiculous.

On the other hand, Tulum is filled with the bones of antiquity. And Elvis loves old bones.